Brenton

Udor

Simone

Desaraux

This is a work of fiction. Any references to historical events; to real people, living or dead; or real locales are intended only to give the fiction a setting in historical reality.

Other names, characters and incidents either are the product of the author's imagination or are used fictitiously, and their resemblance, if any, to real-life counterparts is entirely coincidental.

Copyright © 2019 by Brenton Udor / Simons Publishing

ISBN: 9781092292924

All rights reserved. No part of this book may be used or reproduced in any manner whatsoever without written permission, except in the case of brief quotations embodied in critical articles and reviews.

Printed in the U.S.A.

udor.brenton@gmail.com

For Rose

No one has made a greater mistake than he who did nothing because he felt he could do only a little.

~Edmund Burke

Simone Desaraux

Chapter One

The distraught young woman gripped the dying man's hand tightly against her bosom as she wept. She sat uncomfortably on her legs while the man stared up at her from the hard cobbles of an obscure Paris alley. The two were surrounded by a number of uniformed *Sûreté Nationale,* several of whom, with drawn weapons, were diligently searching the bowels of the dark corridor for any signs of the assailant who had a short time ago stabbed a knife into the man who lay bleeding on the ground. Another squatted on the other side of the wounded man with both of his hands overlapping each other as he pressed against the hole in his chest that was oozing more blood than the pressure was stopping.

"Has someone called an ambulance?" the woman shouted up at the nearest *gendarme.*

"*Oui,* one has been dispatched and is on its way," the uniformed officer replied.

"Simone ..." the wounded man croaked as he squeezed the young woman's hand harder.

"*Oui, père*, they are coming to take you to *l'hôpital* ... hang on, please, for my sake ..." the young woman tearfully replied.

"No, no, *ma fille*, my daughter ... I fear this is my last case. I go to join your mother soon.

"No, papa ... stop speaking like this, save your strength. You're going to be fine ..."

"Listen to me, Simone," the dying man urged over the protest of the officer trying to hold him still, "you must take up the chase for me, do you understand? You must catch this animal and bring him to justice before he destroys any more lives ... do you hear?"

"Papa, stop, the ambulance in coming, you're going to be all right," she pleaded as the sound of the sirens droning off in the distance were getting closer every second.

"Chase him down for me, Simone," her father sputtered, as blood formed a pool in his mouth. "Simone ... I ... I ..."

"He has stopped breathing, move aside," the officer ordered her, as other men now hurriedly knelt down and attempted to assist.

Simone quickly rose, stepped back a few paces, and watched helplessly. Unable to fully control her emotions she clenched her fists in anger and wept freely. Finally, the officers shook their heads in chorus and stood up, just as the ambulance pulled into the mouth of the alley with its lights flashing. The attendants came running forward and examined the injured man only to confirm what the other police officers already knew. The time of death was announced and written down; the body was covered with a sheet, placed on a stretcher, and then slid into the back of the ambulance. A moment later it left the way it had come.

Simone now stood alone and numb as she leaned against the wall of the dirty alley for support. Her cold, blood stained hands, were buried into her trench coat pockets as she watched the ambulance, carrying her now dead father, drive away from the crime scene.

"He was a superb *détective*," a man's voice suddenly announced from behind her. Instinctively she spun around into a crouch, both hands outstretched, as she held the Walther P38 that was now pointed at the man behind her. The other policemen in the alley shouted at her in warning, but the man waved them away after he issued a few quick orders.

"*Inspecteur en Chef?* I beg your pardon, *Monsieur*, I did not know it was you," she apologized and quickly put her weapon away.

"No need for that *Détective Desaraux*. No apology will be expected tonight. You have lost a father and I have lost one of my best men, and a good friend," he replied, coming over to her. She embraced the older man around the neck and began, again, to cry freely.

"There, there, Simone," the inspector consoled. "We will get to the bottom of this, I promise you. Come now, I will escort you to your home."

The next day Simone Desaraux entered the office of a very tired looking Police Chief Inspector Jean Pierre Russo, who sat behind a large cluttered desk in his shirt sleeves, drinking black coffee, and reading reports.

"Come in, Simone. Please sit down," he said courteously. "Can I get you something to drink ... coffee perhaps, *oui?*"

"You can get me the murderer of my father," she said bluntly as she plopped down heavily into a chair.

"Have you slept? Have you eaten?" the inspector asked gently.

"Have you? You look as though you have been here all night."

"*Qui*, I have been right here trying to figure out how to proceed," he replied, tapping a finger on the papers strewed across the desk top.

"And?"

"And this man we are after is a *fantôme*, a ghost ... your father knew this when he took the case years ago when you were a child."

"And last night?"

"Last night was the closest your papa, or anyone on the force for that matter, has ever gotten to him ... but ..."

"But it wasn't good enough, was it? He saw my father coming and he murdered him in cold blood ... like a dog," Simone replied, trying to manage her temper.

"Like so many others, I regret to say. We will get him, Simone, I promise you," Russo consoled.

"*I* will get him," she blurted and stood up, "*I* will hunt this pig down and bring him to French justice. It will either be the noose, or a bullet from my gun, I swear it," she shouted angrily. Simone's outburst caused a young officer to poke his head inside the office and asked if everything was all right.

"Yes, yes, Raymonde, everything is good. Now, find me a lead on this killer and bring more coffee," the senior official ordered, waving him away.

"*Qui, Chief Inspecteur,*" the embarrassed officer replied, and then quickly closed the door.

"I apologize, *inspecteur* ..." Simone began.

"No need, I find it difficult myself to maintain control. However, if we are to get this man, then we need to do it smart ... use our brains and not our emotions. Now, here is what I propose for the time being ... that you go home before you do something unprofessional in your grief and I have to suspend you from duty for becoming a liability to this department. That would surely break my heart. You have my word that we will work day and night to find this murderer. As soon as I know something, I will tell you. And then there is the funeral that must take place, with full honors of course ... will you be able to *maintenir votre sang-froid*, maintain your composure for that?"

"*Qui, inspecteur,* I will not embarrass my father's memory, my department, or you, sir."

"I have confidence that you will not. Now, go home, Simone, there is nothing more you can do here today."

"But sir, I have other cases and ..."

"Not today, detective, your head is not in the game. Now, you are dismissed, *au revoir.*"

Simone Desaraux snapped a salute, turned, and left the police station.

When she arrived back at her apartment she kicked off her heels and desired a stiff drink. But then sadly realized that it was too early in the day for alcohol, which made her feel even worse, and she didn't smoke.

"Mon Dieu, peut-être que je devrais commencer?" she said into the empty room, but she didn't want to start any bad habits now ... her papa would not have approved. She pinched the bridge of her nose to try to drive away the despair and the anger she felt on being so helpless. "I will find him and ..." she began to say, until she was interrupted by the telephone. She went over and answered it.

"*Allo*," she said into the receiver.

"*Détective Desaraux?*" a man's voice said on the other end.

"*Oui*, who is this?"

"Let us just say that I am a concerned citizen in the matter of your father's untimely death."

"Who is this? What are you saying, *monsieur*? What do you know?"

"What I know could very well put this murderer into your hands if you would be willing to compensate me for my information."

Simone cursed into the receiver. "You, *monsieur*, whoever you are, are a pig if you think you can bribe an officer of the *sûreté*. If I discover where you are, I will arrest you for attempted bribery and interfering with an ongoing investigation, do you understand?"

There was no reply on the other end of the line, just heavy breathing for a long time.

"I am hanging up," Simone threatened. "Pray I never meet you. I keep my promises."

"I believe you, *détective*," the voice responded. "I was just curious if you are truly your father's daughter, *fidèle* ... loyal, and I perceive that you are. And so, I will divulge to you the whereabouts of the man who murdered your dear papa."

"You ... you know this beast?"

"I'm afraid so. We were, shall we say, business associates, until he became the animal that he apparently is. I no longer owe him my protection. He has become a stain to this city and needs to be dealt with."

"Then tell me, *monsieur*, tell me his name and where I can find him."

"When I knew him he went by the name, Andre Canard, but I am certain that is not his real name."

"Andre Canard ..." Simone whispered.

"*Oui, détective.*"

"What does he look like? Describe him to me."

"He is a man of medium build. When I knew him he was grey haired and clean shaven. He has a notch taken out of the top of his right ear. He said it happened when he was a child, something involving a family pet."

"Where do I find him?"

"Ah, *détective*, where does one usually find a rat ... the sewers."

A location was given and then the line went dead.

"*Allo, allo,*" she barked into the receiver, but the voice was gone. Simone quickly telephoned the inspector and told him what had just happened.

"Come down here at once. I will gather some men and we will find this man whatever it takes," he told her.

"On my way," Simone replied, slamming the phone down, grabbing her purse, and hurrying out the door.

When she arrived at the police station there were at least thirty heavily armed officers waiting next to a line of vehicles with the motors running. Chief Inspector Russo was hurrying down the stone steps along with some others when Simone approached.

"*Magnifique*, you have arrived just in time," he said to her. I have called ahead and had that entire block sealed off, and every exit from the sewers covered. Leave your auto and ride with me," he added as he pointed to the back seat of one of the waiting cars. "No sirens, *comprendre?*" he shouted at his men.

"*Oui, inspector*," replied a chorus of voices as everyone, plus equipment, stuffed themselves into the row of cars. A moment later the inspector's car, taking the lead, pulled away at high speed down the street.

The location was a pre-revolution stone building at the end of an alley that was now used as an entry point to the immense network of the city's sewers. Simone and Russo were the first to enter the small building where a municipal worker was already being detained and questioned. He said that two men had arrived earlier and one used his telephone. Then they went down the steel gangway into the sewer.

"Describe them for us," Russo ordered. The nervous employee gave a fairly close description of the man, Andre Canard, who Simone immediately recognized from her phone conversation with the informant.

"It is him, inspector," she said.

"Very well. I wish you to remain here with this man and question him further. I will take some of the *officiers* down and see what we can find. There rest of you seal off any exits for two city blocks," Russo ordered.

"*Oui, inspector,*" several of the officers responded and then left.

"I am coming with you," Simone objected.

"The sewers of Paris are no place for a woman ..."

"But, sir ..."

"Simone, I have already lost one *détective* and friend this week, I do not wish to lose his daughter as well. You will follow orders and remain here. If I find him, or if I need you, I will send a man back to fetch you, *comprenez vous?*"

Simone cursed quietly under her breath but reluctantly nodded.

"*Oui, inspector.*"

"*Bon* ... and by the way, I see that you have not lost your dear father's talent with profanity," Russo smiled.

"*Excusez-moi*," Simone apologized.

"Never mind ... wish us luck," Russo said, and then he left through a metal door with half a dozen armed officers behind him.

"*Madame*, am I under arrest?" the city worker asked, looking very worried.

"No. And it is *Détective*," Simone corrected. "Now, if you would, explain to me, in detail, what transpired when the two men arrived here."

After an hour elapsed, Simone was becoming agitated.

"I don't like it," she said to one of the officers, a sergeant, standing in the room with her.

"I don't either. What do you want to do? You are the ranking officer."

"You," she said, addressing the city employee, "go home and tell no one what is happening here," she ordered.

"*Oui, detective*," the man replied, visibly relieved, and scurried out.

"Now, sergeant, I want you and some men to come with me. I intend to go down there and find Inspector Russo."

"*Oui, detective,*" the officer replied.

A few minutes later, Simone and four *policiers* entered the Paris sewers with flashlights and weapons.

"Which way, *détective?*"

"I believe they would go right ... stay alert," she responded, and then trudged into the dark water, her short boots and nylons now soaked with the smelly ooze of the flowing stream. After a few more yards they came to a platform with a stone landing. They climbed up the few steps provided and then their flashlight beams located a door on the other end.

"Look there," Simone pointed.

"Let us be careful," the officer cautioned.

Simone held out her pistol, focused her light on the door, and carefully moved forward. When they reached the door she ordered the men to open it. The door led to a narrow passage that snaked off to the right.

"Let's go, *soigneusement,* carefully," she said. Her men followed.

It wasn't too very much longer until they all heard shouting ... and then gunfire, echoing in the distance.

"We will go ahead of you," the sergeant insisted as he, and two other armed men, pushed past her and ran ahead. Simone cursed and tried to keep up. When she arrived she found herself in a stone room facing the backs of a small crowd of policemen as they huddled around something. Simone's heart sank with the thought of the inspector ...

"Inspecteur Russo," she shouted.

"I am here, *détective*. Let her through," he replied. The men parted revealing Russo on his knees next to a body.

"Is it him? Did you kill him?" Simone asked, looking down at the man.

"No. But, I believe this is your *informateur*," Russo said looking up at her.

"How do you know?"

Russo held up a small card with writing on it.

"Is this not your exchange, hmm?" Russo asked.

Simone took the card. Written on its surface was her phone number as well as the name: Andre Canard, followed by a brief description.

"*Oui*, this is what I was told ... this must be the man on the *téléphone*. What happened here?"

"Quite simply put, it was an ambush. I believe, meant for you, Simone. Also, there were others, at least two. One was shot and fell into the flow ..." Russo said, pointing to an opening in the wall several feet from them where there was a ledge. Below was a large pipe gushing fetid water that cascaded several feet into another channel. "My men are trying to find the body as we speak."

"And the other?" Simone asked.

"He ran off with my officers at his heels. This man, however, spoke a few words of interest to us before he succumbed to his deserved wounds."

"What did he say?"

Russo stood up and brushed his hands off. "I encouraged him to cleanse his conscience while he had the chance. He said that the beast Canard has left the country."

"Left France, for where?"

"America ... San Francisco to be more precise ... and it would seem he has a head start."

Chapter Two

Metropolitan Police Chief D. Richard Clifford sat behind his overly cluttered desk, chewing on a cigar, and talking on the telephone. When he was finished he put the receiver down and ran a handkerchief across his forehead.

"Great, this is just what we need …" he grumbled colorfully. "Fay!" he barked at his office door. Almost immediately a good looking woman dressed in a blue uniform and sporting sergeant stripes stuck her head inside the office.

"You bellowed, Chief?"

"Yeah, I did. Locate McCormick and get him in here, pronto," Clifford ordered.

"You know, Chief, we have intercoms now, right there next to your coffee mug … all you need to do, like I've shown you, is push the little red button on the thing and

I'll hear you at my desk, right out there," she pointed with her thumb behind her.

"Why do I need a blasted toy, when I can just yell for you like I've been doing since you were a rookie?"

"Lord, I don't know, boss, it's only a new decade and we live in a modern world," Fay replied dryly and rolling her eyes.

"Modern world my ... By the way, did you take your exams yet?"

"You mean for Detective? No. My mother's been sick and I ..."

"There's nothing wrong with that woman," Clifford scolded and pointed a finger at her. "Schedule the exam or I'll do it for you, got it? Now, find Shawn McCormick for me ... dismissed."

"You got it, boss ... and, uh, thanks for the nudge," Fay grinned.

"Yeah, forget about it ... and bring me some more coffee when you get a-chance," Clifford grumbled, waving her away as he picked up some documents to exam.

Private Investigator, Shawn McCormick entered the police station, shook a few hands of former fellow officers that recognized him, and then headed for the office in the back of the place.

"How's it goin', Fay?" he asked as he approached her desk.

"Swell, Shawn. How's Maxine feeling?"

McCormick pushed the hat back farther on his head. "Big as a house, according to her. She says if her belly button sticks out any more she's gonna have me hang-a warning light on it."

They both laughed.

"The poor thing," Fay replied. "You tell her if she needs anything, just call me."

"Can ya rub feet?" McCormick asked.

"I rub my mother's. I'm an expert," Fay laughed. "Now, you'd better get in there," she pointed with her thumb towards the office door labeled, 'Chief of Police'. "I just gave him a refill, but he's chewing nails about something or other."

"Okay, Fay, thanks," McCormick said, and then he walked in.

"About time you showed up, Mac, I really need you on this one," Clifford said as McCormick stepped into the office. "Hey, how's Max today?"

"She's good, Chief ... cranky, but good. So, what's goin' on anyway?"

"Pull up a chair and I'll tell ya."

McCormick took off his hat and dropped it on the corner of Clifford's desk, and then plopped down in one of the chairs in front of it.

Clifford placed both arms on top of the desk and leaned forward. "Believe it or not, I just got off the phone with the Police Commissioner, who gotta telegram earlier from, and get this, an inspector in France who wants our help."

"France?"

"You heard me. It seems that one of their murderers has skipped the country and is headed this way."

"I don't get it, why come here?"

"Ya got me swingin' ... all I was told was to cooperate with the detective they're sendin' over here to help find this guy and deport him back to Paris for trial."

"Like we don't have enough of our own crimes to solve?" McCormick asked.

"Yeah, tell me about it. That's what I told the commissioner. But he told me, in no uncertain terms by the way, to cooperate with this Frenchman and promote 'international good will with our foreign counterparts', whatever that's supposed to mean."

"Sounds like he's runnin' for mayor," McCormick yawned.

"Matter of fact he is, next year. So look, I got enough to do just keepin' the streets safe from *our* murderers around here. And, as you know, with the case load on our detective staff, plus budget cuts, we're stretched pretty thin these days. Mac, I need you to handle this on behalf of the department. How 'bout it?"

"Well, I've been tryin' to keep my own case load light because of Maxine ... you know, stickin' around the house as much as I can?"

"Yeah, I get it, and I don't blame ya, but could ya baby sit this French character and help us catch this guy? You know, 'international good will'?"

McCormick shook his head and chuckled. "Sure, Chief, why not, any case files on the wanted man?"

"Nothin' right now until this Frenchy gets here. I guess he's got all the information."

"And when's that supposed to happen?"

"He's in the air right now, or so I was told. I'll let you know when he lands."

"Fine, boss," McCormick said, standing up. "I'm gonna head to the office to tidy a few things up, and then I'm headin' back to the house. Max wants to go shopping, again, for baby stuff."

Clifford chuckled. "I remember those days ... glad they're over too. Enjoy it while you can, McCormick, they grow up and leave home before you know it."

"Uh, let's not get ahead of ourselves. The kid isn't even born yet." McCormick replied. Then McCormick buried both hands into his trouser pockets. "Ya know, I still can't believe this is happenin'," he said, shaking his head back and forth.

"Mac, I remember you saying that up at the lodge on your wedding day. As far as this baby is concerned, you'll believe it at three in the morning when it's diaper changin' time," Clifford laughed.

"Yeah, you're probably right," McCormick replied with a laugh. "Well, I'd better get. See ya later, Chief."

Simone Desaraux

"Okay, Mac, and thanks again."

"Hey, don't thank me yet. Wait 'till you get my bill," McCormick said before shutting the door.

After speaking with Fay briefly, McCormick left the building and headed for his car. When he got in, something occurred to him.

"Hope this guy speaks English," he said out loud. "Oh, well."

McCormick started the car, checked his mirrors, and then pulled away from the curb.

Chapter Three

Detective Simone Desaraux carried a single suitcase out of the terminal and onto the sidewalk where she spotted a waiting police car. She walked over to it, put her suitcase down, and knocked on the driver's side window.

"Yeah, lady, how can I help ya," a burley officer asked.

"*Allo,* I am *Détective Desaraux.* You are expecting me, *oui?*" she said with a heavy accent.

"Huh? *You're* the French detective?" the surprised cop replied.

"*Oui* ...that is, yes. Now, may I have transportation to my *un hôtel, s'il vous plait?*"

"Uh, yeah, sure lady ... hang on a second," the cop replied as he looked at his partner, who shrugged his shoulders. "I'll call it in," he said, picking up the police radio's microphone, adjusted a knob, and then saying: "This is twenty-one at the airport, we got the visiting detective here, how do ya want us to proceed ... over?"

"Detective McCormick is on his way ... orders from the chief ..." the dispatcher replied.

"Got it. Twenty-one out. Okay, lady, somebodies comin' to get ya. Do ya wanna sit in the back?"

"Uhh, Charley, that drunk we put in the tank a little while ago, remember he puked back there? I don't think they cleaned it up very good, ya know?" the other cop said.

"Is that what that smell is? Fer cryin' out loud I thought you were gonna switch out squad cars ... fer the love of Pete ..."

"Never mind, *officière*, I will wait right here, *si cela ne vous fait rien*," she replied.

"Huh?"

"If you don't mind?" she quickly translated.

"Oh, no, no... No problem, lady," the cop smiled.

"It is *Détective*," she corrected.

The two cops looked at each other and then both smiled up at the attractive brunette standing outside of their car. It wasn't long before a black Cadillac pulled up behind the squad car. A tall, handsome man, dressed in a suit and trench coat, got out and walked over.

"Glad you could make it, McCormick," the cop in the driver's seat said out his window.

"Got here as quick as I could, Mike. So, where's our visitor?"

The cop motioned with his head to the other side of the car. The other cop got out of the passenger side, picked up the woman's suitcase, and smiled widely at McCormick.

"Yer kiddin' me?" McCormick announced.

Both cops laughed out loud. The the one holding the suitcase came around the back of the squad car, handed it to McCormick, and then gave him an exaggerated wink.

"So, how's that baby comin' along, huh, McCormick?" he smiled.

"Fine, Charley, and don't be a wise guy. Who's the dame?"

"She's the French Detective."

"Yer kiddin' me?" McCormick repeated.

"*Excusez-moi, monsieurs,* but I speak very good English," the woman said as she came over. "I am Détective Simone Desaraux and we have much work to do. So, if you are here to take me to my *hôtel*, please do so. I am very tired," she said, sticking her hand out to McCormick who took it and gently shook.

"Nice to meet ya," McCormick replied, and then he went over to his car, opened the trunk, and placed the suitcase inside. Afterward, he opened the passenger side door for her.

"Private Detective Shaw McCormick at your service ... welcome to America," he smiled and pulled on his hat brim.

Simone nodded courteously, walked over, and got in. After McCormick shut the door the two cops laughed again, gave McCormick the thumbs up gesture, and more exaggerated winks.

"See ya 'round, McCormick," they joked.

"Yeah, yeah," McCormick replied and waved them off with his hand before he slid into the driver's seat and shut his door.

"Idiots ..." he muttered as he started the car.

"You do not respect your men, *monsieur*?" Simone asked looking surprised.

"First of all, they're not my men," McCormick answered as he pulled away. "Second of all, I've known those two guys for years, they're good cops ... they just like to kid around?"

"I am sorry ... 'Kid around'? *Qu'est-ce que c'est?* What is that?"

"Yeah, you know, pull your leg ... joke around ... you know?"

"If you are meaning they are trying to make you look *insensée*, foolish, *oui,*I understand this. It was *évidant* to me."

"Oh really? How's that?"

"Neither they, nor you, nor your superiors, I suspect, were expecting a woman to be sent here. I also *deduce* that your friends were attempting to make you feel guilty seeing as you are a married man who is *attendre un enfant.*"

"Huh?"

"I mean, expecting a child."

McCormick gave her a sideways look of surprise. "How do ya know that? We just met."

"It is quite simple, *monsieur*, you wear a wedding ring, and there is a package of cloth diapers in your back seat."

McCormick laughed and nodded his head. "Well, looks like I'm the idiot and you're the detective. However, I'm not clairvoyant either, so where're we goin'?"

"Ah, *oui* ... my *hôtel* is called *Les Bras Coloniales*"

"The which?"

"Pardon, it is the Colonial Arms.

"I know where that is, we'll be there in a jiffy."

"Jiffy? What is 'jiffy'?"

"Soon as I can get you there is what I mean."

"*Bon*. Now, I have a question. You have mentioned that you are a *détective privé*, that is to say, a 'private detective'. You are not with the police department?"

"I was a cop and a detective on the force for years. I went private a little while ago ... doing okay too, so far," McCormick replied.

"But how will you arrest this criminal if you are not a policeman?"

"Tell ya what, lady, why don't we worry about finding and catching the guy first, okay? Besides, I'm sure I can talk him into coming along quietly when the time comes."

"*Mon Dieu,* they have sent me a fool ..." she said under her breath as she pinched the bridge of her nose.

"Hey, I speak pretty good English too, sister, and I also have good hearing. So, what's your problem?"

"First of all, I am not your *soeur* ... your 'sister'. And my problem is, *monsieur*, amateur private détectives who think they can operate within the realm of law enforcement ... we have them in France. They believe they are, how you say, the 'Sherlock Holmes' or some such nonsense."

"Like I said, if you were listening, I was a detective on the police force for years. I know the job and I'm pretty good at it, or so I'm told, and so do my commendations. And don't forget, you're in my town now, not Paris, understand?"

"*Oui*, I understand," she said, now turning her body to him. "And *you* need to understand that *mon père* ... my father, who was also a decorated *détective*, chased after this killer for most of his career, right up until this monster murdered him in a filthy alley in Paris," she blurted angrily.

McCormick looked over at her as a single tear ran down her cheek.

"I'm sorry, detective, I didn't know. But look, I gotta say I'm a little surprised they would send you, of all people, over here after this guy."

Simone turned back around and stared out her side window long enough for her to retrieve a lace handkerchief from her purse and dab her eyes with it. When she finished she cleared her throat and looked out the front window.

"My Chief Inspector and I have a long history ... besides being my superior on the force; he is also my Godfather, and a close friend to my late father. They had served together for many years and were an inspiration to me to become a *détective*. If he would have refused to send me, I would have come on my own, and he knows this. And so, I am here with his blessing and the support of the Paris police department. Apparently, *détective*, you feel that because I am a woman that I am *incompétent* to perform my duty in this matter ..."

"Hey, I never said that, nor did I imply it either," McCormick objected. "Look, it's just been my experience in this line of work that people like you who've been through some tough times are too close to the problem to be objective, especially in a criminal investigation. It's obvious that your still in grief over the murder of your father and I can't help but wonder what you'll do if you find this guy."

"What I will do, you ask?" she said, glaring back at him. "What I will do, is my duty, *monsieur*. I will offer him the opportunity to become my prisoner to be taken back to France to stand trial. If he refuses or resists in any way, I will empty my gun into him, *élémentaire* ... simple. Either way, I will return to France a happier woman for my trouble and my father will be avenged. Do we understand each other, *détective?*"

"Well, I guess we do now, detective ... and by the way, if we're gonna work together you can call me Mac."

"Mac?" she laughed briefly, "You American's are so very *informel* ... what is word? 'Informal', for my taste ... like your food. However, 'when in Rome', as they say ... And so, since we have been assigned as *les partenaires*, partners, you may call me Simone or Detective Desaraux, you may choose."

"Well, Simone is easier to say than ... Deshraroo?" McCormick replied with a grin.

Simone laughed politely and shook her head.

"Des-are-roe. Simple, *oui*?" she corrected.

"Maybe for you ... anyway, here's your hotel," McCormick said, pulling into the parking lot.

"*Bon,* I could use a hot bath and some decent food, if there is any in this city," she replied, looking outside at her surroundings

"Like French food do ya?"

Simone turned and stared back at him in wide-eyed disbelief. McCormick immediately recognized his faux pas and chuckled. "Sorry, dumb question. How do ya feel about old world Italian?"

"I enjoy Italian cuisine. Do you know of a suitable place?"

"Indeed I do. I'll give ya the address as soon as we get you checked in, how's that?"

"Thank you ... err, Mac? Is that correct?"

"That's fine, let's get you inside."

Chapter Four

After a bath and a short nap, Simone took a cab to *La Palazzo Ristorante* on Rivera Boulevard. She was surprised to see evening gowns and tuxedos entering the place and wondered if her simple black dress would be appropriate for the surroundings. She clutched her purse which held, besides currency, passport, and her police I.D., a loaded Walther P38. She soon dismissed any misgivings when the noise of her tummy's cravings interrupted her thoughts, and her nose caught a whiff of Italian cooking coming from inside. Setting her jaw she strode from the sidewalk and up to the entrance where a host wearing a black tux greeted the guests.

"Welcome to La Palazzo, *signorina*," he said with an Italian accent and bowing slightly. "Are you expecting guests or will you be dining alone this evening?"

"Just myself, *merci beaucoup, monsieur*," she replied with a smile.

"Ahh, you are French! Excellent, we seldom receive visits from French speaking guests. Is this your first time in San Francisco?"

"Yes, I am here on holiday," she lied, "and I'm *affamato*," she added in Italian

"Oh, no, no, we cannot allow that," the host tsk-tsked, "at least not here at La Palazzo ... come, *signorina*, let me find you a table," he said, waving at a waiter standing nearby. After giving him instructions, Simone was whisked away to a corner table just off the main dining room, but within eye-shot of the bar. After she ordered her food she also asked for a glass of red wine. It was brought to her promptly, along with some condiments, by someone who looked remarkably like a character you would only see in a gangster movie. Simone looked surprised as she stared up at the man standing at her table.

"May I help you?" Simone asked.

"Nah, I just wanna to make sure yoos comfortable," the stocky, much older man, replied. "My name is Sal Canale, and I run this place. If yoos need anythin', just ask for me, *capice?*"

"Thank you, *monsieur*, I will keep that in mind," she replied graciously.

"Enjoy your dinner," Sal said with a slight bow, and then walked away into the barroom. When he reached the bar, he asked the bartender to bring up the telephone from behind the counter. Sal dialed and let it ring, until …

"Mac? Sal. That French dame you warned me about is here at the restaurant … Hey, she's a-looker …. Yeah, I'll keep an eye on her for ya … And listen, I also got my boys keepin' an eye out for that Frenchy mook she's after. If he's hit town, we'll find him … Hey, no problem …. Yeah, *ciao*."

Sal hung up the phone and motioned for the bartender to put it away. Then he sat on a bar stool and watched Simone for a few minutes admiring the view … that is until a non-descript male guest walked past her table, stopped, turned around, pulled out a gun, and pointed it at her. Simone saw the weapon and expertly rolled out of her chair just as the assailant fired, boring a jagged hole in the plaster wall behind her.

"Gun!" Sal yelled. The bartender quickly responded, and a shotgun appeared in his hands as frightened patrons ducked and scrambled to get out of harm's way. He tossed the gun to Sal who rushed a few feet to where Simone lay sprawled on the floor just as the gunman prepared to take another shot. Sal didn't waste another second, he opened fire, blowing a large hole through the edge of a wall and spraying the gunman with pellets. By this time several men, built like refrigerators, rushed into the room brandishing weapons. The wounded gunman fired at them, hitting one in the shoulder.

"Get that guy!" Sal shouted. With that said, the men mercilessly opened fire, point-blank, at the gunman who took most of the rounds center-mass ... he fell to the carpeted floor, quite dead. Sal dropped the shotgun and rushed over to Simone amid the screams of distressed patrons trying to exit the building as fast as they could.

"Hey, kiddo, you okay? You hit?" Sal asked.

"No, no, *monsieur*, I believe I am unharmed ... thank you," she replied as Sal helped her to her feet.

"Hey, we try to take care of our customers ... good for business, ya know?" Sal smiled crookedly despite the close call.

"Who was that man?" Simone asked as she tried to control her breathing.

"Why don't we go see, uh?" Sal said, putting and arm around her waist and bringing her over to the bullet ridden body that Sal's men were now guarding.

"Gino, close the kitchen for the night and make sure the parking lot is clear when the cops arrive, *capice*?" Sal said to one of the men.

"You got it, Sal, the man replied and then quickly left, while several others stood around brandishing weapons.

"Turn 'em over," Sal ordered another one of his men, who, using his foot, turned the body over onto his back.

"You know this mook, lady?" Sal asked, Simone.

Simone shook her head. "I've only just arrived in this country. I do not know anyone."

"Ya know Shawn McCormick, don't-cha?"

Simone shot Sal a suspicious look. "*Oui*, I know the *détective* … how do you … Who are you, *monsieur*?"

"Let's just say that Mac and I are old acquaintances … and he was worried about ya. Looks like he had good reasons too, huh? Tell, ya what, why don't we get you to my office in back and wait for the cops, looks like we got some explainin' to do."

"Mac … yes, I understand now. *Merci*, I mean, thank you, and your people, for saving my life."

"It's all on the menu, sweetheart. Now, I'm gonna let Bruno here walk ya's through the dining room to my office and he'll stay with ya. I need to hang around here 'til some blue show up. You gonna be okay?"

"Yes, I will be fine, thank you," she replied, although shaking as she brushed the food debris off the front of her once clean black dress.

"Good, I'll send you some food and vino from what's left in the kitchen ... can't have you starve in my joint after missin' a bullet now can we?" Sal joked.

Simone smiled and then gave Sal a grateful peck on the cheek.

"Merci beaucoup," she said, and then she followed Sal's man out of the room.

"Cute kid, huh, Sallie?" one of the other men said.

Sal nodded. "Yeah, a real winner that one ... Go get-a table cloth and cover up this jerk," Sal directed, pointing at the body, "looks like business is a bust tonight."

A little while later the police arrived, along with Chief Clifford and McCormick, who, after taking statements from Sal and a few others, went to Sal's office where a very large hood stood guard outside the door. When they walked in Simone was voraciously stuffing the last bit of a meatball sandwich into her mouth. She smiled as best she could as she chewed and then washed it all down with a hearty gulp of red wine.

"Hey, you okay?" was the first thing a concerned McCormick asked.

"*Oui*, I am. I was, how you say, 'starving' ..."

"He means are you injured?" Clifford interrupted brusquely.

"No, *monsieur*, as you can see, no holes in my new dress," she replied, holding up her arms, " ... and besides, I have been shot at before," she added, and then poured herself the last of the wine from the now empty bottle, shaking the last drops into her glass, before raising it up in salute at the two men and then gulping it down. "It is not French, but it will *juste avoir à faire,* just have to do ..." she slurred, giggled, and then hiccupped. "*Excusez-moii,* she apologized.

"Oh swell, she's drunk," Clifford observed, pushing the hat back on his head.

"She's hammered all right," McCormick agreed. Then Sal walked in.

"How's our pretty guest doin'?" he asked.

"She's drunk," both McCormick and Clifford said in unison.

"Huh? Guess I should'a sent her a smaller bottle," Sal replied, mildly embarrassed.

"And there is my hero," Simone said loudly as she stood up, went over to Sal, and draped herself around his neck. "You will receive *La Médaille de Bravoure* ... that is to say, the medal of valor for having saved the life of an officer of the *Sûreté*," she slurred and then saluted.

"Detective, I need a report on what happened here tonight, pronto," Clifford growled.

Simone stiffened, turned towards Clifford, and looked him up and down. "And you are this man's papa, *monsieur?*" she said pointing her thumb at McCormick.

"His what?" Clifford barked, causing Simone to jump.

"Take it easy Chief, she's drunk and prolly tired from the flight," McCormick said in her defense.

Clifford took a large step forward until he was nose to nose with Simone. "Detective, I'm Police Chief D. Richard Clifford and as long as you're in this country, you work for me, got it? So sober up and give me a report," he thundered at her.

Simone's eyes widened and her mouth hung open. "*Inspecteur en Chef?* I, I am sorry, I did not ..." Then her eyes rolled back into her head, and she spiraled downward with all three men easing her flight to the floor by rushing in to catch her.

"We ain't gonna get much outta her tonight, Chief, and I don't think its safe back at her hotel room either," McCormick said as he held her head in one hand.

"Yeah, yer prolly right," Clifford agreed.

"She can stay at my place," Sal offered. "We got plenty of rooms and I got the man power to keep her safe until she sobers up ... with that much wine in her, I'd say tomorrow afternoon sometime. What'da yas think about that?"

Both Clifford and McCormick nodded.

"I'll send-a squad car over here tomorrow to bring her to the precinct for debriefing. Thanks Sal. Now, I'd better get outta here with that dead body and see what we can find out about him ... see ya later, McCormick, Sal," Clifford said as he swooped out of the room.

The next afternoon Simone awoke in a strange bed with a doozy of a headache. She noticed she was still in her black dress as she flipped back the covers and tried to focus on where she might be. What arrested her immediate attention, after her head cleared enough, was the sight of white porcelain behind a half-opened bathroom door ... and she wasted no time in making a bee-line for it. Afterward she left the room, without shoes on, and careful crept down an elegantly carpeted hallway.

"This is not *mon hôtel*," she muttered to herself as she passed decorated walls lined with expensive oil paintings. She stopped momentarily to look at one, a *Monet*, when she suddenly heard a woman's voice from behind her.

"Good afternoon."

Simone turned and saw a young woman dressed in a maid's outfit. "Why don't you grab your things and follow me, please," she invited.

"Where am I? What is this place?" Simone asked as she walked back towards her bedroom.

"You have been the guest of Mr. Salvador Canale. Now, please follow me, there are people waiting to speak with you downstairs."

Simone went back inside, splashed some water onto her makeup starved face, did her hair up, grabbed her purse and shoes, and followed the maid downstairs to a comfortable office where Sal and McCormick were waiting.

"Come in and have a seat, detective," McCormick invited.

"How ya doing today?" Sal asked from behind his desk.

Simone uncomfortably cleared her throat. "I believe I am fine. However, I feel like a fool for my *amateur*, that is to say, unprofessional conduct of last evening ..."

"You're apologizin' for dodgin' a bullet?" Sal remarked.

"No, no, I mean for my conduct afterward ... with the wine ..."

"Mac, do you know what this pretty lady's talkin' about?" Sal asked McCormick.

"Haven't got the slightest idea, Sal. Maybe you just had a bad dream, detective?"

Simone stared in disbelief at the both of them.

"Anyway, now that your awake, I'm here to bring you down to the station so we can figure out what happened last night at the restaurant. So, if you're ready to go, we'll drop by your hotel on the way so you can change," McCormick said.

"*Merci, détective.* I believe I owe you and your Chief Inspector an explanation," Simone replied.

"Just 'Chief' will do, Simone," McCormick corrected and then motioned towards the door. "Thanks, Sal, I'll be in touch," McCormick added as he stood up.

"No problem, Mac ... And, hey, if yas need somebody ventilated on the young lady's behalf, jus lemme know," Sal laughed.

McCormick grinned, nodded, and then left the residence with Simone.

Chapter Five

"International relationships between police departments my backside," Clifford growled at the woman standing in front of his desk, dressed in a smart, grey business suit. "I would've appreciated being given a heads up that your people were sending us the daughter of a murdered French detective as an investigator. I don't enjoy these kinds of surprises."

"*Oui*, I understand your displeasure, sir, but I want to assure you that as a *détective*, I am as *dévoué*, I mean, 'dedicated', as any man on your police force, and I will do my duty in assisting however and wherever I can to apprehend this criminal and bring him to swift justice," Simone replied courageously.

"Oh, do you now?" Clifford responded, unconvinced. "Well, Detective Desaraux, *that* remains to be seen. And I'll tell ya somethin' else, if I find out that you're here on some kinda personal vendetta, I'll kick your back-side across the ocean so fast you won't need an airplane to make the trip, understand?"

"*Oui, Inspecteur en Chef,*" Simone snapped to attention and saluted.

"Stop that. It's just Chief or boss, pick one. And don't salute, this isn't the army. Now, sit down and give me a report about what happened last night at *La Palazzo.*"

A moment later, there was a brief knock at the door and McCormick entered holding a coffee cup.

"C'mon in, Mac, we were just gettin' started," Clifford said.

"Yeah, so I heard," McCormick chuckled, and then handed Simone the cup.

"*Merci,* détective, but I do not feel like coffee at this time."

"It ain't coffee, just drink it down, it'll make you feel better," he replied, pulling up a chair and dropping his hat on the corner of Clifford's desk.

Simone stuck her nose into the top of the cup and sniffed. "*Qu'est-ce que c'est?* I mean, what is this?"

Clifford leaned forward and jabbed a finger at her. "He said drink."

Simone quickly gulped down the warm liquid. Immediately her head and body aches miraculously disappeared.

"*Mon Dior,* what *is* this?" she remarked in surprise, handing the empty cup back.

"Feel better?" McCormick asked, taking the cup and putting it next to his hat.

"*Oui,* thank you."

"Good, now let's hear all about your little adventure last night. We already have Sal's statement along with a few others," McCormick said.

Simone cleared her throat and began. As she related events, Clifford wrote. When she was finished, he looked over at McCormick.

"No doubt in my mind, Chief," McCormick said, "this guy, whoever he is, is in town and he's connected. Looks like we just might have a little more than a fugitive to track down."

Clifford sat back in his leather chair and looked up and the ceiling. "This is just what I need, a crime wave," he grumbled.

"*Excuse moi,* I do not understand what is happening? Who was this man that tried to kill me last night?" Simone asked.

"Simone, your friend apparently knows you're in town lookin' for him and he hired a hit man to take you out of the picture," McCormick replied.

"*Excusez-moi,* he is *not* 'my friend' ... and I do not understand? How does he know I am even here in this country?"

"Detective, this guy probably knew it when you boarded the plane in Paris," Clifford said to her. "Now, here's something you most likely don't know either. This fella you're after is connected, probably internationally, and it looks like he's made himself comfortable here in our city."

"*Connecté?* So, is it you are saying he is involved with *crime organisé?*"

"If you mean organized crime, yeah, somethin' like that," McCormick said while he browsed through a file that Simone had brought with her. Then he cleared his throat and handed it back to her. "This is all in French."

"*Oui,* I know ... I will be happy to translate the information to you."

"Well, little lady, start translatin'," Clifford ordered.

"Very well," she replied, and then cleared her throat again. "I shall begin by stating that the majority of the information in these reports with regard to this criminal was compiled by my late father. This beast ... this man, had no name ... that is until recently, which was given to us in a Paris sewer by a dying man who was, by all evidence, a close associate of this killer. He told us his name was, Andre Canard."

"Do you believe him?" McCormick asked.

"Traditionally in France a dying man's statements are considered trustworthy. However, Andre Canard may be a false name this criminal is using at present. But now I am curious. You had mentioned that this man, Canard, is part of a gang in your city? How do you know this for a certainty?"

"We'll explain that when you're finished fillin' us in on the history of this guy ... continue, detective," Clifford urged.

"Bien sur, monsieur... of course. It all started when I was a young girl. My father was called in to investigate a murder in *Corbeil-Essonnes*, a suburb of Paris. It was a particularly gruesome affair, as I remember my father speaking of it, but it was only the beginning."

"Beginning of what?" Clifford asked.

"The beginning of a series of murders that would span two decades."

"So, we're talking about a mass murderer?" McCormick asked.

"*Oui,* this man is believed to have killed a dozen or more people, both men and women ... at least this is what we know so far. There are perhaps more victims. My father became obsessed with this man because of what happened to his good friend and former partner who was found dead in his home, along with his wife.

After the investigation, it was concluded that they were, indeed, the latest victims at the time of this beast, Canard, and it was verified by a note delivered with my father's friends watch attached to it. The note read: 'Stop trying to find me or your daughter is next.' I remember the day as if it were yesterday when my father sent me away to boarding school because of this.

Ma mere, that is to say, my mother, died when I was very young and my father was overly protective of me. I stayed at the school until I was eighteen, and then I entered the *école de police*, the police academy. During this time more murders occurred and my father never rested from his attempts to hunt down this man. Finally, two weeks ago, this animal killed my father in an alley in Paris and we learned later that he had fled the country to this city."

"Sorry for your loss. Now, what can you tell us about this killer?" Clifford asked.

Simone continued, "According to the investigation, he was fairly young when he began his career ... perhaps in his twenties ..."

"So, he'd be somewhere in his forties by now?" McCormick added.

"*Oui* that would seem reasonable, however, it is only an estimation. This man is also very ... what is word, *méticuleux?*"

"Meticulous. So he's careful?"

"*Oui*, no *prevue*, evidence, ever. No finger prints. We also believe he covers his shoes with perhaps socks ... he leaves nothing behind that we can trace. It is maddening."

"Tell us about the disposition of the victims?"

"*Je ne comprends pas?* I am sorry, I mean, I do not understand your question?

"I mean how they were killed?" McCormick pressed.

Simone moved uncomfortably in her seat. "The men were knifed in the chest, and then ..," she paused.

"And then what?" McCormick asked, leaning forward.

"The French detective swallowed with difficulty before answering, "and then a *trophee* was taken."

"A trophy? What kinda trophy?" Clifford asked.

Simone cleared her throat. "*Une oreille* ... an ear, usually the right one," she replied, visibly shaken, as she touched, briefly, the right side of her head.

Clifford looked over at McCormick who sat back and slowly shook his head. "Yer not kidding, right?" he asked.

"No, *monsieur*, I mean, Mac, I wish it were not so," Simone replied. "Even *mon pere*, my father, was not spared this *indignité*."

"I'm sorry." McCormick said softly, placing a hand gently on her forearm.

"*Merci*, but I am all right. Let us please continue," Simone replied bravely.

"What kinda sick nut are we dealin' with here?" Clifford blustered ... And then, "Fay, Coffee," he barked at the office door.

Clifford's desk intercom suddenly came to life. "*Push the red button, Chief,*" came a staticky reply.

"Never mind the fancy gadgets, bring coffee in here, pronto," he barked again. "Uh, detective, do you need anything?" Clifford politely asked, Simone.

"*Qui*, Chief, *café* would be most welcome," she replied with an appreciative smile.

"That's two coffees, Fay, pronto," Clifford hollered again.

A moment later the office door swung open and Fay entered with two steaming mugs of coffee, one in each hand. She handed one to Simone and the other she placed on the blotter in front of Clifford.

"Anything else, boss?" Fay asked, putting a hand on her hip and snapping her chewing gum.

"No ... and hold all my calls and any visitors. Dismissed," Clifford replied briskly.

Fay nodded and began leave, but then she unexpectantly leaned over Clifford's desk and held up a single index finger in front of Clifford's nose. After making sure she had his attention, she placed her finger on the bright red button sticking out of the front of the new intercom unit sitting just to the right of Clifford's elbow.

"Just one tiny push, Chief, no bellowing, got it?" she said as she flexed both eye-brows at him.

Clifford rolled his eyes. "Woman, you're worse than my wife," he huffed, taking a worn toothpick out of his white shirt pocket and shoving it into his mouth.

Fay stood up straight and smoothed out her uniform.

"I'll take that as a compliment, Chief," Fay smiled smugly.

"Yeah, beat it," Clifford growled under his breath.

Fay turned, and after briefly asking McCormick if he needed anything, she exited the office and locked the door behind her.

Simone looked at both men, not quite sure of what to make of what just happened. Then she took a drink of her coffee. She placed a hand over her mouth, closed her eyes, and she swallowed hard.

"Too hot?" Clifford asked, sipping on his own mug.

Simone shook her head slowly as she placed a free hand, momentarily, on her forehead.

"I know how you feel, detective," McCormick chuckled, "when my wife first tasted that stuff, she said it was like drinking motor oil."

"I would have to agree," Simone replied, coughing slightly, as she stared at the hot, black liquid in her mug.

"Okay, breaks over, let's get back to what you know about this Canard lunatic," Clifford said, looking seriously now at Simone.

"*Oui*, Chief," she said, gripping the mug in her lap tightly. "The attacks on the victims we have deduced were unexpected and violent. It is believed that the *trophée* was taken while the victims were still mostly alive."

McCormick cleared his throat and re-crossed his legs.

"What' da ya thinkin', Mac?" Clifford asked.

"Same thing you are … up close and personal. Whoever this guy is, he's bold, and not afraid of being caught. Now, Simone, where did these murders take place?"

"A variety of locations … city, country, in private homes, hotels, public parks, alleys."

"Time of day?"

"Seldom during the day… usually at night or early evening … like a vampire."

"What about his female victims? Any form of …"

"No. None of them were molested to my knowledge, at least according to the autopsies."

"Killed the same way, were they?"

"No. All of the female victims were *étranglé,*"

"Strangled?"

"Oui."

"With?"

Simone took a gulp of her coffee before answering. *"Une garrote.* Autopsies suggest a wire, or cord of some kind. He apparently wears gloves, and we have deduced that he is quite strong. The throats were crushed with considerable bruising on the surface of the skin. And ..."

"And what?"

Simone cleared her throat. *"Les chaussures des femmes ..."* she rattled off.

"Hey, slow down. English," McCormick encouraged.

"Excusez-moi," she apologized, "the women's shoes where *endommagé ...* damaged."

"Damaged? What'da ya mean, damaged?" Clifford asked.

"The toes of both shoes were *écorché ...* oh, what is word?"

"Skuffed?" McCormick suggested.

"*Oui,* what you said," Simone replied.

"What's your point, detective?" Clifford asked.

McCormick exhaled, "Chief, I think what she means is the evidence suggests that this guy's female victims were pulled off their feet, like they were being hung. Drawing the conclusion that this guy is strong, am I in the ball park, detective?"

Simone nodded. "*Oui,* you are correct. That was also our *evaluation.* Although I am not sure of what a 'ball park' has to do with the case?"

"Never mind that for now. His victims, what's the ratio of men to women?" McCormick continued.

"More female than male. Also, none of the victims, as far as we could determine, knew or were related to each other."

"Except you father's friend, remember?" Clifford corrected.

"Oh, *oui*. That was, of course, the only exception," she replied.

"And the ear?"

"The same for all of his victims," Simone sighed.

"Sounds like a crime of opportunity and need to me," McCormick said.

"*Oui*, we are in agreement, *détective*. This creature is a predator, he needs to kill to satisfy a hunger. He is like *Jack l'éventreur* ... the Ripper, the British murderer who roamed the streets of London looking for his next victims. Canard has done the same in Paris, and now he is here. I would watch *les morgues*," Simone said.

"Well, we already got one guy in the morgue," Clifford interjected.

"Yeah, but somethin' else," McCormick reasoned. "This Canard is not only a predator, but he's also involved in organized crime. Probably like you said, Chief, 'international' I'm guessin', from the way he got somebody as soon as he landed here to put a hit on the detective here."

"So, what is your *theorie*?" Simone asked.

"My theory is this killer, at present, is no street thug. Now, maybe he started out that way, I dunno, but from what that police report probably says, and what you're tellin' us, this guy's got some smarts to outwit your father and the French police all these years and leave no trace. I think we're looking for a man that's highly intelligent, sophisticated, and has got some real pull in the underworld. And I also think that's where we need to look for him ... find his associates, put some pressure on 'em, and they'll point him out."

"You seem overly sure of yourself, *détective*, when the best France has to offer could not track him down," Simone answered, turning her body to him.

"Well, if you've gotta better idea, detective, let's hear it?" Clifford replied.

"No. No, I am afraid I do not ... at least for the present time," she sighed, and then placed her coffee mug on Clifford's desk.

"Good, then we'll follow McCormick's lead in this. Any objections?"

Simone sat back, took a deep breath, looked at Clifford, then over at McCormick, and said, "No, boss."

"See that, she's gettin' the hang of it here all ready," Clifford remarked. "Now, anything else you got that might help us find this guy?"

They talked for another half-hour or so picking Simone's brain for any further details until finally Clifford stood up.

"All right, we've got plenty to go on for right now. Thank you, Detective Desaraux. I'm putting a uniform outside your hotel room, don't bother to object, and I'm placing you in McCormick's custody as far as this investigation is concerned. You have no peace officer status in this country, so if any arrests are to be made, McCormick will take the lead."

"Well, Chief, officially I can't arrest anyone either, remember? I'm private and ..." McCormick began to object.

"You got cuffs, McCormick?" Clifford interrupted.

"Yeah."

"Well then if you need to arrest somebody, haul 'em in here and I'll take care of the politics. I want this guy off my streets, you two got that?"

"Yes, Chief," they both replied in unison.

"Fine. Now beat it the both of ya's. Lemme know as soon as you get a break on the case. That's it," Clifford said in dismissal.

They both stood up to leave. Simone started to salute, hesitated, and then walked towards the office door. McCormick reached over to take his hat off the desk when Clifford mouthed silently to him: "Mac, keep an eye on her." McCormick nodded, turned, and followed the French detective out.

Chapter Six

The two detectives got into McCormick's car and drove away from police headquarters.

"Where do we begin?" Simone asked.

"Well, fortunately, I know some folks who have connections to the criminal underground ... you met one of 'em last night?" McCormick replied as he weaved into traffic.

"You are speaking of *Monsieur* Canale, *oui*? I suspect he is what you would call 'a gangster'?"

"Yeah, but this gangster's on our side. I put a bug in his ear about this case and I'm anxious to see what he's come up with. So I thought we'd stop by his place and find out. I gotta hunch."

"*Excusez-moi,* but why would you place an insect into someone's ear?" Simone asked innocently. McCormick looked over at her and chuckled.

"Sorry, that's good old American slang for I gave him a hint about something ... a hunch I had at the time, get it?"

"A hunch?"

"A suspicion."

"Ah, *oui,* I understand now ... although it is going to take me some time, I fear, to understand all of your colorful American sayings."

"Well, you seem to speak the lingo pretty well. Where'd you learn English anyway?"

"At boarding school. The nuns were insistent, since the Americans were allies during the war."

"Makes sense. Anyway, I suspect that if we can find out what mobsters this guy's in bed with we can shake 'em down for information, and that's where our pal Sal Canale comes in. He has extensive connections in this city's underworld. Maybe he can do more good than me kicking in doors."

Simone insisted that McCormick translate into plain English what he just said as the two drove to *La Palazzo.*

Once they arrived they entered the restaurant through the service door around the side of the building. Once inside they were greeted by several cooks who pointed the couple through the kitchen, and then gave them directions to one of several small, private, dining rooms on the premises. When they entered the dining room they saw, seated at one of the tables, Nicky Beonverdella, co-owner of the place.

"Heya, Nick, how's it goin'?" McCormick said in greeting as the two moved towards the table.

"I'm feelin' better today, Mac ... come sit down. Say, who's the pretty dame? Ya didn't trade Maxine in on a new model, did ya?" Nicky joked.

"Nah," McCormick chuckled, "Nick, lemme introduce you to Detective Simone Desaraux on loan to us from France," McCormick said, holding a chair out for her to sit.

Nicky looked Simone over greedily with his one good eye, the other, if he had one, was obscured by a black eye-patch. He smiled and extended a hand to her. She gave McCormick a quick, apprehensive look, but then accepted Nicky's hand. When she did, Nicky brought it to his lips and respectfully kissed the top of it. Then he spoke to her in fluent French. Simone seemed pleasantly surprised as the two carried on a brief conversation until

Sal Canale walked into the room, followed by two refrigerators wearing pinstripe suites.

"Good, everyone's here," Sal said, and then he turned to the two goons that came in with him. "I want the room secured, *capire?*"

"You got it, Sal," they replied, and then they left to stand outside the two entrances.

"I didn't know you spoke French, Nick?" McCormick said.

"Ah, yeah, pop insisted that I get educated in the romance languages when I was a kid ... made me take Latin from the nuns, ya know?" Nicky replied, adjusting the vest under his suit jacket.

"I to have had a similar experience as a child," Simone added.

"So, you're a detective like McCormick, huh? How's that workin' out for yas?" Nicky asked.

"At the present time, *monsieur*, I am attempting to track down the murderer of my dear father and of so many others. I hope you can help."

"Yeah, we can help with that, can't we Sallie?" Nicky replied looking over at the older man.

Ya know, I think we just might be able to. We've got pretty good at takin' care of guys who kill people's fathers, right McCormick?"

McCormick nodded slowly and looked as though he was momentarily remembering something unpleasant. "So, what'da ya have for us?" he asked.

Sal pulled out a chair, sat down next to Nicky, and then he leaned in.

"After that little event last night at the restaurant, Nicky and I are real anxious to find the mooks behind the hit on this little girl here," Sal began, reaching over to pat Simone's hand. "Now, I made some discrete calls and, low and behold, somebody who knows somebody said that there's some guys in town tryin' to re-invent *La Lancetta Rossa.*"

"*La Main Rouge?*" Simone repeated in disbelief.

"English," McCormick urged.

"The Red Hand," Sal answered.

"Never heard of 'em," McCormick said.

"As well as you should not," Sal replied, holding up an index finger. "That bunch is a little before your time ... fact is, if Don Carmine were still here, he'd tell ya all about 'em."

"*Excusez-moi, monsieur* Sal, but are you saying that Andre Canard is somehow part of this gang?" Simone asked.

"It's looking that way, kid," he replied.

Simone nodded slowly in understanding. "I am familiar with them, *monsieur*," Simone said, "I recall reading about this gang in my academy days as well as my father speaking of them."

"Okay, so who are these guys?" McCormick asked.

"They began in France after World War I," Simone continued, "at first as part of the resistance against the Germans. However, later they turned to crime ... smuggling arms, contraband, drugs, and so forth. Then they disappeared, as least as far as the French police were concerned. Then Interpol was established in 1923 and renewed efforts were made against them."

"You are correct," Sal added, "Interpol went after these guys like nobody's business."

"So how was Don Carmine involved?" McCormick asked. "Oh, by the way ..." McCormick turned to Simone, "Don Carmine was Nicky's dad and he ran 'the family business', if ya get my drift, in this town for years, that is until .... well ..."

"It's okay, Mac," Nicky replied. Then he addressed Simone. "He died last year. He kept the mobs in check in this town for a long time, and Sal and I hope to keep it that way."

"And the police department appreciates it too, Nick," McCormick added.

"I see. Please go on," Simone encouraged.

Sal nodded and continued "Anyway, these Frenchys ... oh, no disrespect to you, detective, thought they could come to this country and run their business here. They tried in New York, Detroit, Los Angeles, and here, especially seein' as how we have a seaport and a railroad. However, these mooks didn't understand 'the rules', and so Don Carmine, and the rest of the families, corrected that mistake real quick. We ran 'em right outta town and back to France ... that is until now it seems."

"Yeah, I'll say... right under our noses too. We must be gettin' old, Sallie," Nicky lamented.

"Not too old to take care of these guys movin' in on our territory. And now to make matters worse they send in muscle to our restaurant for a hit? This is war," Sal replied in subdued anger, rapping on the table top with his knuckles.

"Hey, look, Sal, I know how ya feel, but we don't wanna start a war with these guys quite yet. At least not until we get this Canard character that the detective here is after," McCormick interjected.

Sal held up both hands. "We understand this. So, for now, we will make the necessary inquiries to find this man who killed this pretty girl's daddy. After that, the gloves come off."

"Ya know, I can't help but wonder why they would be stupid enough to send a hit man here? Why not wait until Simone got to her hotel room?" McCormick said.

"That would have been more discrete, more *professionale*," Simone agreed.

"Yeah, don't they know who runs this joint?" Nicky added.

Sal sat back and scratched the side of his face in thought for a few moments. "Unless somebody's tryin' to send a message," Sal said.

"That's stupid," Nicky replied, "who'd wanna start a war with us, huh?"

"Yeah, maybe, but let's think about it," McCormick said, "let's say you start a war, which starts a crime wave ... the crime wave involves the police and the mobs ...

everybody is distracted, and if everybody's distracted then ..."

"This beast can hunt without detection," Simone finished for him.

"That's right. Just chalk it up to another victim of a mob war. The police would be so involved in fighting the gangs they probably wouldn't think twice about a single killer on the prowl ... maybe ... but, look, this is only a theory," McCormick said.

"It's plausible," Sal agreed.

"Okay, say I'm right, this is all the more reason to keep a lid on this until we know more," McCormick said.

"In other words, you'd rather we didn't start shootin'?" Nicky said.

"Yeah, Nick, that's exactly what I'm gettin' at."

"We can do that, for the time being, can't we Sal?" Nicky replied.

Sal nodded reluctantly, but added. "If they hit some of the other families, I can't be responsible for what happens, *capire*?"

"I understand, Sal, and I don't expect you to. This is all the more reason to find this guy quick and take him outta the equation," McCormick said.

"So, where do we begin?" Simone asked.

"Any ideas, Sal?" McCormick said, looking over at him.

"Yeah, I gotta good idea, why don't the three us go visit Manie Stracuzzi," Sal replied.

"Ain't he in the joint?" Nicky asked.

"Sure is, and doin' twenty to life, if I remember right," McCormick added.

"Yeah, but even in the joint Manie's an ear, he knows what's goin' on. If there's a new gang in town, he'll be wise to it and maybe give up some information about 'em ... provided of course we ask politely, you understand?" Sal said.

"By politely, you mean a bribe?" McCormick asked.

Sal chuckled, "Somethin' like that. But you leave that to me," he replied, standing up. "So little lady, you wanna go for a ride?" Sal smiled over at Simone.

"Sure she does," McCormick answered for her as he also stood.

"*Excuse moi*? Where are we going?" Simone asked.

"Alcatraz prison."

Chapter Seven

The barred, steel door slammed closed behind three visitors. Escorted by an armed guard, they walked down a dank, stone hallway and finally into a room with a metal table bolted to the floor, surrounded by several chairs. The guard looked at the three with an expressionless face, but then nodded and pointed to the chairs.

"Take-a load off, detective, we'll bring your guy in shortly," he said.

"Thanks," McCormick answered as he pulled out a chair for Simone.

"This ain't no place for the likes of her," the guard said looking at the pretty woman.

"She's also a detective, here on official business," McCormick replied.

"Yeah, well, it don't make it right ..." the guard grumbled and then stepped out of the room.

Simone sat down uncomfortably and rubbed her arms as if she was cold.

McCormick and Sal sat down on either side of her.

"Don't they have prisons in France?" McCormick asked.

"*Oui,* France has very good prisons, some centuries old and infamous. Why do you ask?"

"You don't seem comfortable here, which surprises me since you're on the police force and ..."

"Do not presume that because I am a woman that I cannot handle this situation. This is not new to me. I have arrested and escorted many criminals to *la geôle* ... the jail ... it is just, how do you say, the 'goose skin' does not stay away, *comprendre?*"

"Yeah, we get it ... no worries, right Mac?" Sal said.

"Fine with me. I'm just glad that the Chief got us in here so quick. Me not being on the force could-a been a problem getting us permission to see this guy," McCormick said.

After a few more minutes the door reopened and a guard walked in. He was followed by two others with someone in between them wearing hand cuffs and leg irons. The guards hustled the prisoner over to a chair across the table from the three visitors and pushed him down into it. Afterward, two of the guards left, leaving one standing by the door. What the three visitors saw was a middle aged, balding man with a two day old beard and a tooth pick sticking out of his mouth. No one said a word as the prisoner surveyed each one of his visitors in turn while he chewed on the small piece of wood between his yellow teeth. Finally, looking at McCormick, he spoke.

"Well, you're a cop alright," he said in a low, rough voice.

"Private dick," McCormick simply replied.

Then he turned his attention to Simone. "And you're beautiful."

"Hey, knock that off," Sal warned, jabbing an index finger at him.

"And it's nice to see you too, Sal," the prisoner replied with a slight chuckle. "What'da ya want, huh? You lost or somethin'?"

"Manie, I, that is, *we*, need your help with a certain matter," Sal replied calmly.

"My help?" Manie responded with over exaggerated surprise, "Sal Canale needs *my* help, does he?"

"Yeah, that's right," Sal said.

"Where were you and Don Carmine when the cops threw my life away, huh?" Manie suddenly barked, as he slammed his handcuffed hands on top of the table causing Simone to involuntarily jump.

"Hey, settle down or I'll work ya over," the guard responded, slapping the heavy baton he was holding against the palm of his other hand.

"Yeah, yeah ..." Manie grumbled colorfully and then slid back in his chair. "So, what's the dame doin' here, huh? You're not gonna tell me she's one of mine are ya?" he laughed.

"Manie, any offspring you've ever had are crawling in the sewers, let's get that straight," Sal replied abruptly and pointing a finger at him. "And as far as Don Carmine was concerned, you got caught all by yourself 'cuz you were stupid ... that ain't like you ...

"Yeah, so I got caught ... Maybe I needed the vacation, so what?" I got it good in here.

Sal leaned forward and put his arms on the table top.

"Sure ya do, tough guy. All right, look," Sal continued, "we got wind that there's some new players in town, maybe tryin' to set up shop. We wanna know what you've heard. How 'bout it?"

Manie laughed and slowly shook his head. "You gotta be kiddin' me. You came all the way out here to ask me about a gang?"

"Not just any gang," McCormick interjected, "the Red Hand. You heard of 'em?"

Manie stopped laughing and began to chew on his toothpick. Then he cleared his throat.

"How'd you hear that name?" he asked suspiciously.

"Somebody who knows somebody said somethin'," Sal replied.

Manie looked up at the ceiling. "I might've heard somethin', and if I did what's in it for me, huh?"

"You help us and maybe we find a way to get you put in a minimum security joint," Sal whispered.

Manie looked seriously at Sal. "You can do that?"

Sal sat back and folded his hands over his tummy. "You would be surprised. Now speak."

"Hey, I'm an ear, ya know? I ain't never put a bullet in anybody ... and they stick me in this place ..." Manie grumbled.

"So talk and change your scenery. What'da ya know?" Sal replied.

Manie looked over at the guard and then back at Sal. Sal understood and motioned with his thumb for the guard to leave, which he did without hesitation. Once the room door was closed and locked, Sal cleared his throat and nodded to Manie.

"I see you ain't lost your touch," Manie complimented.

"Just spill it," Sal replied impatiently.

"Yeah, okay ... So, there's a guy in the joint with me here and we's talkin' and he tells me about these guys ... foreigners, who are movin' stuff through town ..."

"Stuff? What kinda stuff?" McCormick asked.

"He didn't say and I didn't ask," Manie replied. "Anyway, this guy tells me these other guys are truckin' whatever it is down from Canada to here and then shipping it out overseas. That was then. Now, recently I hear about these same guys ... You mentioned the Red Hand?

"Yeah, we did. Is it them?"

"That's the name that was dropped ... and listen, even in here you keep yer trap shut and that name off your lips, unless you wanna wake up with a shiv in your neck."

"Tough bunch, huh?" McCormick asked.

"Yeah, tough and smart ... or so I'm told," Manie replied.

"Okay, so where do we find these mooks?" Sal asked.

Manie rubbed his face with his hands. "I dunno ... but maybe I can find out *if* your playin' straight with me about gettin' me outta here and into minimum. How 'bout it?"

"You work on this for the family and I'll figure out the transfer. You just do your part, *capire?*" Sal said.

"Yeah, yeah, I get it ... so gimme a few days," Manie replied. "Now, I'm curious, what's the lady doin' here?"

"This lady's a French cop who's lookin' for the man who killed her daddy. We think he's part of this Red Hand gang," Sal said.

"Is that so? French cop huh? Tell ya what, sweet thing; I'll keep an ear out for him, no extra charge, how's that?" Manie leered.

"Okay, we're done," McCormick said, standing up. "Guard."

The guard reentered flanked by two others. They escorted Manie out of the room and left the door open.

"Well, now we wait and see," Sal said. "Let's get outta here."

Chapter Eight

The dark sedan moved slowly down the narrow, back city street, while the fog rolled in around it, as if by command, to obscure any recognition of what was about to happen. The sedan stopped just behind another parked car that was sitting there idling. After a minute or so, the two drivers got out, eye-balled each other, and then went to their respective rear passenger doors. Opening them, they waited for their passengers to disembark into the swirl of mist that surrounded them. The two unknown passengers got out, stepped a short distance away from the autos, and then moved carefully towards each other. When they were a foot or so apart, they stopped and waited. Finally, one spoke.

"So, you're the French guy, huh?" a man said in a thick Italian accent. He was short, stocky, and typical of his Sicilian heritage, with dark eyes and gray streaked black hair under his hat. The other man, who was tall, well built, and wearing a trench coat and hat, simply stood there and said nothing at first, but his eyes covered every inch of his guest as a predator might his quarry before an attack.

"What'sa matter, ya don't speak any English?" the Italian asked, mildly irritated.

"I speak very good English, *monsieur*," the Frenchmen replied with his own heavy accent. "However, I am not here for the entertainment ... your services were engaged to take care of a matter and you have failed, explain," he said flatly.

"Hey, so my guy bungled it, all right? It happens. We'll put a hole in this broad for ya, don't you worry about it ... and no extra charge either, *capire*?" the Italian joked.

The Frenchmen's jaw line tightened. "This 'broad', as you refer to her, is no one's fool. It is my understanding that she now is under the protection of, not only the local police, but a private *détective,* along with one of your local gangsters. I am correct, *oui*?"

"Yeah, yeah ... some private dick named McCormick. And as far as that 'gangster' yer referrin' to is concerned, Sal Canale can't get outta his own way. Him and that idiot kid of the late Don Carmine are behind the times. As far as I'm concerned, it's time for a change in this town ... and that's where you come in, Frenchy, you're gonna make us rich and powerful, aren't-cha?" the Italian chuckled.

"Is that what you imagine our business is all about?" the Frenchman replied.

"Well ain't it? Hey, you wanna set up shop in this town, you gotta play ball with the families or else you can move your operation back to Europe. Now, this is where I come in, see? I'm gonna get you in with the mob that takes orders from me. And I'm tellin' ya, I'm takin' a big risk bringin' outsiders in on our business in this town. The other families won't appreciate it unless I can convince 'em to see things our way, get it? Now, lemme ask ya, what'd you do to this dame to get her to travel all the way over here to put a slug in ya, huh?"

"The matter is *privé*, private," the Frenchman replied as he took out a cigarette case from an inside pocket, removed a cigarette, and lit it up.

"Private, huh? Yeah, well, you gotta understand somethin', pal, as of right now you're business is *my* business, see? I'm not just a hired hit man that takes the trash out for ya. If this broad's gonna complicate things, I need to know why, got it?" the Italian said, shoving both hands into his outside coat pockets and feeling the handle of his .45.

"*Monsieur*, do you wish to continue to do business with me and the people I represent with their extensive international connections or not?" the Frenchman asked quietly, and then he took a long drag on his smoke.

"Look, we was doin' jus fine before you and your guys showed up, and we'll do jus fine if you leave, or get dead ... either way," the Italian replied angrily.

"Very well," the Frenchman sighed. "I killed the woman's father back in Paris."

"Oh, did you now?" the Italian remarked.

"And she's a policeman, a *détective*, no doubt sent over here to find and arrest me for the murder."

"Or blow your brains out," the Italian finished. "So, you had me put a hit on a French cop?"

"*Oui*, I did ... which begs the question, why did you stupidly choose to send your *agresseur*, your 'hit man' to a restaurant run by local gangsters? I wanted this taken care of *discrètement*, discreetly ... in her hotel room. No mess ..." the Frenchman said, flicking away his cigarette in anger. "If I would have known how this was going to turn out, I would have handled it myself."

"Yeah, but ya didn't, and my guy's an idiot, and now he's a dead idiot on a slab in the morgue. Look, I'll handle this. This is my town and we do things different here ..."

"How? By starting a crime wave between competing families? You stupid fool. The last thing we need is to draw attention to ourselves, and to the *opération*, there's too much at stake, *comprenez vous*?"

"Hey, watch your mouth, pal, you asked for my help, remember?" the Italian retorted and shoving an accusing finger at him.

"*Oui*, I remember, *mon erreur*, my mistake, which I fully intend to correct. Right now ..."

A muffled shot came out of the mist and struck the Italian's driver standing by the car, center mass, sending him to the ground.

"What the?" the Italian cursed as he attempted to bring out his weapon ... but too late. The Frenchman had already taken several quick steps forward and had now placed the razor sharp tip of a five inch, bayonet type blade, of a French made flick knife against the windpipe of the Italian's throat.

"Drop your *pistolet, monsieur*," the Frenchman ordered.

The mobster did as he was told. "Hey look, Pal, maybe we got off on the wrong foot, eh? What'da ya say. We need each other, right?"

A fog horn blew eerily in the harbor, cutting through the damp night air. The Frenchman returned to his own car and driver, who was busy loading the first victim into the trunk of the other car. Suddenly, a third man walked out of the fog unscrewing the silencer from the barrel of his gun. He quietly walked up to the Frenchman, nodded, and then spoke.

"Are you alright, *monsieur*?"

"*Oui*. Put the other pig into the auto and then dispose of them both in the harbor, *comprenez vous*?"

"*Oui, monsieur*, it will be done. Anything else?"

The Frenchman looked down at what he held in his gloved, left hand ... a folded, bloody, white handkerchief. He carefully unfolded it, revealing a severed right ear. The man with the gun swallowed hard, but said nothing. The Frenchman, seemingly satisfied with his prize, refolded the handkerchief and shoved it into an outside coat pocket. "Be so kind as to find me another local gangster with more brains than the one I've just dealt with. These American's cannot all be fools. Also, one more matter, have our people locate Detective Desaraux ... apparently I need to take care of her personally."

Chapter Nine

Maxine McCormick sat sprawled in an overstuffed parlor chair watching the Jack Benny show on a new RCA 12" television set. She giggled and snorted at the antics of the characters displayed on the black and white screen, when all of a sudden she was distracted by an annoying cramp in her left hip. She struggled to straighten up, but her swollen belly always seemed to be getting in the way of the simplest movements these days. Suddenly, the child within kicked her a good one.

"Ouch, take it easy, will ya?" she complained as she massaged both sides of her tummy. After taking a deep breath and with some effort, she managed to find a more comfortable position. "Alright, look," she continued rubbing, "it won't be long and you'll be out of me ... and then we'll both get-a break ... at least I hope so. Now, the doctor says we got about another month for you to cook, so just be patient and stop punching me, okay?"

Just then she heard the front door open.

"Mac? Is that you?" she called out.

After a moment McCormick poked his head around the corner of the doorway.

"Hello, cupcake, how're ya feelin'?"

Maxine sighed. "Like I swallowed a bag of cement that's how. So, are you home for a bit?"

"Uh, yeah ... Say, I brought a guest with me, hope you don't mind?"

"A guest? Who is it," Maxine replied, as she tried to sit up.

McCormick motioned with his hand and Simone appeared in the doorway.

Maxine's jaw suddenly dropped. "McCormick, you brought home a brunette? She'd better be the new maid or I'm gonna ..."

"No ... I mean, yeah ... I mean, look," McCormick stammered, "Max, this is Detective Simone Desaraux from France. She's visiting the department regarding a case we're working on," he replied.

"So, she's your new partner? Mac, are you kiddin' me? Of all the ..."

Maxine began cursing like a sailor until ...

"*Excusez-moi*, I did not mean to cause trouble. Perhaps I should go ..." Simone began.

"Max, take it easy, will ya?" McCormick interrupted. Now, I know you're uncomfortable and, no, she's not my new partner, but we are working this case together, Chief's orders ... and beside somebody tried to put a bullet in her last night and ..."

"Somebody tried to kill her? Where? When? Oh, you poor thing, come over here. Mac, be a dear and bring us some tea, will ya?" Maxine said as she held out her hand to the visitor.

Simone gave McCormick a quick, confused, look before crossing the room to sit on an ottoman next to Maxine.

"Yep, that's just what the doctor's been warning me about ... she's just like the weather," McCormick grumbled under his breath as he took off his hat.

"Darling, tea please," Maxine repeated.

"Comin' right up, sugar," he replied, and then headed for the kitchen.

When he returned, Maxine and Simone were both chatting away in fluent French.

"Oh, darling, this poor girl's just lost her father to some creep. I hope you're close to catching him," Maxine said.

"I wish," McCormick replied as he brought over a tray of freshly brewed tea along with several cups.

"Oh, this is the blend I had in your chief inspectors office, no?" Simone asked as she smelled the piping hot brew that McCormick served.

"*Oui* ... I mean yes, detective," McCormick replied as he handed his wife a cup, poured one for himself, and then found a chair to sit down in.

"Oh, Mac, you spoke some French. I think you're rubbing off on him, Simone," Maxine laughed.

Simone smiled and sipped on her beverage. "Your wife is an amazing woman, *détective* ... so full of life and ..."

"Yep, you got that right, sister," Maxine interrupted, repositioning her tummy. "I gotta feeling this little rascal's gonna be a handful when she arrives."

"You mean, *he*, don't you sweetheart?" McCormick smiled.

"It doesn't matter, darling, as long as *she's* healthy," Maxine smiled back, and then they both laughed. "So, Simone, fill me in on this case. I'm so bored being stuck here at home, I'm ready to help anyway I can," Maxine lamented.

"Oh, please, *Madame* McCormick, do not trouble yourself over this matter. You are with child and you need your strength," Simone consoled.

Maxine looked over at her husband and winked.

"Uh, detective, you don't know my wife," McCormick chuckled.

"It's all right, Simone," Maxine laughed, and then grunted noisily as she repositioned herself again, "I'm built like-a tractor. Besides, maybe if I can keep my mind off my belly I won't be so cranky … right, Mac?"

"You'll get no argument from me, sweetheart," McCormick replied, and then he quickly related some of the details of the case.

Maxine whistled. "Sounds like this guy's a real winner. I'm glad Sal and Nicky are helping … I wish I could do more and … and I gotta hit the can. Mac, would you mind?"

"*Excusez-moi?* 'Hit the can'?" Simone asked curiously.

Maxine laughed as her husband came over and lifted her out of the chair.

"*Je dois aller aux toilettes,*" Maxine translated.

Simone laughed in reply and nodded as McCormick carried his wife towards the back of the parlor.

"I'll be back in a flush, Simone, so make yourself at home," Maxine yelled over McCormick's shoulder.

"*Merci*, take your time," Simone waved at the couple as they left the room. Afterward, she stood up and shook her head with amusement as she slowly walked around the large room, examining this or that, until she ended up looking out a window at the street in front of the house. That's when she noticed a car parked behind McCormick's Cadillac. She stood and watched, her detective's instincts now suddenly on high alert. After a few minutes an unknown man, holding a cigarette between his lips, got out of the passenger's side and stepped over to the sidewalk. He held up a camera, snapped a few pictures, threw down his cigarette, and then got back into the car. After another minute the car pulled away and drove off. Once she was satisfied the car was gone she was out the front door. When she reached the sidewalk, she carefully looked up and down the quiet street before walking over to where the unknown cameraman had stood. She carefully looked around on the ground and found what she was looking for, a spent cigarette. She bent down and retrieved it. She examined it carefully, and then smelled it.

"*Mon Dieu,*" she exclaimed to herself before heading back to the house.

When she arrived back in the parlor, the McCormicks' had already returned.

"Simone, we thought you'd left us," Maxine said as her husband arranged a pillow behind her back.

"Yeah, what gives ... everything okay?" McCormick asked.

"*Détective*, I wish to speak with you privately, *s'il vous plait*," she said.

McCormick shot her a concerned look, but said nothing as he walked past her, through the parlor entrance, and into the long hallway leading to the front door. Simone followed until McCormick stopped about half-way.

"All right, what's goin' on?"

"There were two men outside watching the front of this house. One of them *prendre une photo* ... how you say, took a picture, and then they left," she said.

"Did ya get a license plate number?"

"No, they left too quickly. However, I do have this," she said, holding out the cigarette butt in her open palm.

"So?"

"It is French ... not sold in this country. *Détective*, they have found me. And now they know where you live and your dear wife. *Mon Dieu*, I have put her life in danger I fear. I should go away... back to Paris and ..."

"Hey, knock that kinda talk off," McCormick sternly replied and placed a large hand on her shoulder. "Maybe this is the kinda break we need to flush these rats out. You let me worry about my wife. This is not your fault and we're gonna get these guys, understand?"

Simone nodded and managed a slight smile.

"Mac?" Maxine called from the other room.

"Be right there, sweetheart," McCormick announced, and then he physically turned Simone around and gave her a gentle shove back in the direction of the parlor.

When they got back Maxine had a serious look on her face.

"You okay?" McCormick asked.

"No, I'm not okay, ya big lug. So who're the two guys takin' pictures of our house, huh?" she asked as she crossed her arms over her belly.

Simone looked astonished. "You overheard? *Comment est-ce possible*? How is that possible?"

McCormick stood there momentarily rubbing his forehead. "She has real good hearing, that's why. Okay, look, Maxine, we'd better find you and junior a safer location and ..."

"That ain't gonna happen, McCormick," Maxine snapped back. "Now, let's stop worrying about me and use this opportunity to get to know our new friends and flush out this killer you two are after. I'm pregnant, I'm not an invalid."

"But, Maxine, please, you must be reasonable. The man I pursue is evil and dangerous. You must think of your unborn child," Simone urged.

"Evil men, you say? Oh, Really? Where have we heard this before, darling?" Maxine replied looking at her husband, and then she began to laugh out loud as she held onto her stomach. Simone turned to McCormick for some support, but found that he was also chuckling.

"*C'est fou* ... this is crazy, what is wrong with you people?" Simone said, looking perplexed.

"There's nothing wrong with us, detective," McCormick responded, and then he took her by the elbow and politely escorted her over to a couch before sitting down himself. "Look, lemme explain. It's just that Max and I have been through, well, shall we say, some tough spots in our married life and we've managed to survive. This is just another case."

"And, in my condition, I'll have to admit it's inconvenient, but we'll live with it," Maxine added.

Then the McCormicks' went on to summarize for their guest a few of their past adventures, while Simone sat there in wide-eyed amazement. When they were finished she slowly shook her head.

"*Mon Dieu*, most seasoned policeman, I dare admit, have not had your experiences during a life time of service ... and yet you both have managed to escape certain death on numerous occasions. I regret to have doubted you," she said.

"Not-a problem," Maxine replied. "Now, darling, how do you think we should proceed?"

"Well, first off, I need to phone this in to the Chief. He'll wanna know about this new development. Then, we need to move the detective from her hotel to here ... and make it visible enough for whoever's watchin'."

"It appears that the hunters have become the hunted," Simone replied, grimly. "I must inform you that it is against my professional training to put civilians in danger. Now, do you believe your *inspecteur en chef*, I mean, your Chief will agree to this?"

"Civilian?" Maxine repeated and then snorted, "Why I haven't been a civilian since Mac and I got hitched."

"*Excusez-moi*, but what is 'hitched'?"

"Oh, sorry ... Married," Maxine translated.

"I see."

"And to answer the rest of your question, let's find out what the Chief thinks," McCormick said, slapping his knees as he stood up, and then walking over to the telephone sitting on a stand in the back of the room. While he was doing that, Simone asked ...

"So, is this your first *bébé*?"

"Yep, first and last if I can help it," Maxine laughed.

"Your *grossesse* ... your, uh, what is word ..."

"Pregnancy?"

"*Oui*. It has been difficult for you?"

"Not really. It's just that I'm the kinda gal that can't sit still. I need to be doing things. Don't get me wrong, I absolutely love the thought of having this kid, both Mac and I can't wait to be parents, it's just that ... well, I guess I worry about the kind of mother I'm gonna be."

Simone reached over and squeezed Maxine's arm. "I am sure you and Mac will be wonderful parents, do not doubt yourselves for a moment. I just regret that my presence here puts you both in danger."

"Nah, don't worry about it, sister. If we've survived what we have this long, Mac and I don't see this case as being any big deal. Now, lemme ask, you gotta guy back home?"

Simone blushed slightly and shook her head. "I am afraid I am too much devoted to the force to find the time for romance, perhaps later when this case is over. We will see," she smiled.

"Well, we're all set ... I think," McCormick announced as he walked back over to the two women.

"What'd the Chief say, darling?"

"He says he's comin' right over," McCormick answered.

"This cannot be good, no?" Simone asked.

"I wouldn't worry about it," Maxine replied. "The Chief grumbles and yells a lot, but he's good people, you'll see."

Chapter Ten

"Have you all lost your minds?" Clifford shouted.

"Calm down and stop yelling, I think this kid is finally asleep," Maxine shushed.

"Oh, sorry Max," Clifford whispered in apology, coming over to her and placing a hand gently on top of her belly. After a moment he smiled. "He moved."

"*She* moved ... And by the way, Chief, Simone and I will be just fine here. You worry too much," Maxine said.

Clifford took his hand away and shoved it into his trench coat pocket. "It's my job to worry, and don't forget it. Now, I'm gonna put a circle of cops around this place so that a flea won't be able to cross that blue line without getting arrested."

Maxine rolled her eyes. "Oh, that's gonna help lure the bad guys to us now isn't it? Why not just stick-a tank on the front lawn?"

"I can do that young lady," Clifford replied, pointing a finger at her.

"Max, take it easy," McCormick cautioned, "the Chief is only concerned with ..."

"Yeah, yeah, I know, everybody's worried about poor pregnant Maxine ... gimme a break, will ya? Look, we got an opportunity to capture one of these French thugs and find their boss, maybe even this killer himself ... Canard, right?"

Simone nodded.

"Well then let's not blow it. Let' em come right through our front door for all I care and we'll be waiting," Maxine said, bravely.

Clifford looked reluctantly over at McCormick. "Mac, what'da you think?

McCormick wrung his face with a hand. "Well, I'll admit it's risky for Maxine, and it's lookin' like we can't talk her out of it, right sweetheart?"

"You got that right, buster," Maxine firmly replied.

"And besides," he continued, "we got nothin' as far as leads in this case."

"How 'bout Sal?" Clifford asked.

McCormick just shook his head. "Nothin' yet. Look, Chief, like Max said, if these guys come around then maybe we can capture one of 'em and pump him for information. I say we take some precautions and go for it."

Clifford rubbed the back of his neck while he chewed on a tooth pick. "I'm tellin' ya right now, I don't like it, but I'll agree provided Maxine stays behind a locked door when any trouble starts."

"Hey, wait-a minute," she objected.

"No discussion," Clifford barked. "I don't want my godson to be put in harm's way. Now, we do this my way or I fill the place with uniforms, your choice."

Maxine sighed heavily. "Fine. Have it your way. And it's god-*daughter*," she grumbled.

"We'll see," Clifford replied. "Now, I'm goin' out to the car and order the black and white that came with me to circle the block and then take off. I'll be right back."

Clifford left, while McCormick went over to a cabinet and took out a gun.

"You packin' Simone?" he asked over his shoulder.

"Packin'?" she repeated.

"*Avez-vous une arme à feu?*" Maxine translated.

"*Oui*, I have a *pistolet*," she replied, taking out the Walther P38 from her coat pocket.

"Nice piece. Let's have a gander," Maxine said, holding out a hand.

"You know how to use a gun?" Simone asked as she reluctantly handed Maxine her weapon.

Maxine smiled and wrinkled up her nose as she expertly discharged the loaded clip from the bottom of the handle, and then pulled back the slide, ejecting a single bullet which she caught in mid-air. She checked the barrel briefly, replaced the bullet into the clip, and then slapped it back into the handle. Then after twirling it once around an index finger she tossed it back to Simone.

"It's a cute ladies gun, and I notice it hasn't been fired much. Nice piece though," she said.

Simone just stood in front of her, wide-eyed, as McCormick came over and handed his wife a loaded .45 automatic.

"There's my baby," Maxine said as she accepted the weapon, "come to momma."

"You're ... *bébé?*" Simone asked.

"Well, yeah. A gal's gotta be able to protect herself and her loved ones," she smiled in reply and rubbed her tummy.

"*Mon Dieu,*" Simone sighed.

Maxine laughed. "I know, I take some getting used to, just ask, Mac."

"Amen," he replied and then he bent down and kissed her. "You be careful, wife, understand?" he whispered.

"Of course, darling, you know I'm a real careful girl," she cooed into his ear.

"That's what I'm afraid of," he sighed.

A few minutes later Clifford returned carrying something wrapped in an old blanket under his arm.

"All right, I've dismissed the patrol out front. Now, Maxine, upstairs, pronto."

"Upstairs? What'da ya gonna do, Chief, lock me in my room?" she complained.

"McCormick will you do the honors or shall I?" Clifford said looking over at him.

McCormick nodded and then went over and scooped his wife out of the chair.

"Mac, this ain't fair, ya big lug," Maxine protested.

"Quiet down cupcake or you'll wake the kid," he said as he carried her to the back of the parlor and up the stairs.

"Detective," Clifford addressed Simone.

"Yes, Chief?"

"You watch the street, I'll be right back," Clifford said as he followed the couple.

"*Oui*, Chief," she saluted.

"And don't salute," Clifford barked as he left.

Simone looked at her hand briefly after she removed it from the side of her head. Then she checked her weapon, walked over to the front parlor window, and peered outside. It was late in the afternoon and the sky looked like rain, as thick clouds began rolling in along with the rumble of thunder in the distance. After a few minutes McCormick and Chief Clifford returned, spoke privately to each other, and then Clifford left the house without speaking to her.

"You okay?" McCormick asked Simone.

"*Oui*, I am fine," she replied as she watched Clifford car pull away from the house. "So, we are on our own then?" she asked.

"Yep, looks that way. Tell ya what, I'm gonna go make us some sandwiches; Max is hungry, as usual. I'll be right back. Keep-a lookout."

"*Oui, détective*," she replied as she returned her gaze back to the street in front of the house just as the first drops of heavy rain began to strike the window pane. "*Bon sang*, just what we need," she said under her breath as she looked out. After awhile, McCormick came out with a tray of food and tea. He gave Simone a sandwich and a cup of tea, and then he went upstairs to serve Maxine. Simone ate standing up as she continued her vigil. By this time the sun had gone and the heavy rain storm was obscuring any clear vision of the street. Even so, Simone pressed her nose against the glass as she thought she saw something slowly moving down the street and then stop. It appeared to be a van, but she couldn't be sure due to the now heavy downpour beating against the glass. She turned around to see if McCormick had returned, but she still found herself quite alone. A few moments later, she felt a gust of fresh air enter the room and she knew the front door had been forced open.

"*Mon Dieu,*" she said under her breath as she spun around, bringing her weapon up just in time to see an armed man, dressed in black, appear from around the corner of the doorway ...

"*Déposez votre arme!* Drop your weapon!" she shouted, but the intruder opened fire. Simone dropped to one knee and returned fire, hitting the assailant, center mass, and sending him backward into the hallway. He was immediately replaced by several others who did not hesitate to begin shooting. Simone felt something hot graze her right shoulder as she fired back. Seeing she was outnumbered she began to desperately crawl on her hands and knees to the rear of the parlor where there were several large overstuffed couches. She managed to duck behind the nearest one as bullets thudded into the thick cushions ... that's when McCormick came running down the stairs. He leaped over the banister before reaching the bottom, landed hard, and then crawled over to join Simone behind the couch. They both began to return fire as best they could over the top of the couch as more intruders seemed to materialize out of nowhere to join in the assault. McCormick managed to wound one of them in the exchange, but there were simply too many guns shooting back for either of them to acquire a solid target.

"You, hit?" McCormick managed to ask as he shot blindly over the sofa.

"It is nothing ... I fear we are trapped," Simone replied bravely as she reloaded, feeling fresh blood trickling down the outside of her arm.

"How many are there?" McCormick asked.

"Too many ..." Simone replied with desperation in her voice.

Then suddenly, all hell seem to break loose from above them as hot brass began to rain down as it poured out of a blazing Thompson sub-machine gun that was spraying lead towards the other side of the room. Maxine stood on the stairs in a bathrobe, her back pressed firmly against the wall while the Thompson jumped and roared in her grip.

"*Laissez-nous sortir!* Let's get out," one of the men shouted as the whole group of assailants fell over each other in panic trying to make it to the hallway. Several died on the spot in the hail of machine gun fire as it mowed down its fleeing victims. After few more seconds, the battle was over. Simone and McCormick turned and looked up. Maxine blew a lock of hair away from her face, and then rested the stock of the smoking Thompson on her hip.

"Well, are they gone?" she asked calmly.

McCormick cautiously stood up, weapon at the ready, and went over to check ... there were four dead in the room and one in the hallway. He went to the front door that was swinging in the wind, quickly looked around outside, and then shut it. When he returned, Simone was busy examining the bodies.

"Well, are they gone?" Maxine repeated.

"Yeah, sweetheart, they're gone ... you okay?"

"Nope, I gotta pee," she replied, and then she put the machinegun over her shoulder and went back upstairs.

"You need help, honey?" McCormick called after her.

"No!" Maxine hollered back.

At this a disheveled Simone sat down heavily on the floor next to one of the dead assailants and began to laugh uncontrollably. McCormick came over and stood over her.

"What's so funny?"

Simone stopped laughing momentarily, looked up at him, and then began to laugh even harder as she held up both hands.

"I'd better call this in ... be right back," McCormick said as he headed for the telephone. Before he reached it, he stopped and turned around ... "You sure you're okay?"

Simone continued to laugh and wave him away.

Chapter Eleven

Chief Clifford stormed in with a dozen or so heavily armed uniforms behind him. When he reached the parlor entrance he saw the corpse of an unidentified man bleeding on the carpet. He stopped, cursed, and then entered the larger room. He looked around in disbelief at the bullet riddled walls, furniture, ceiling ... and bodies.

McCormick! Maxine!" he hollered, fearing the worst.

"In here, Chief," McCormick's voice answered from the kitchen.

"All right men, spread out. I want every inch of this house and the grounds checked, move," Clifford ordered his officers.

"Yes, sir, Chief," the cops responded as Clifford headed for the closed kitchen door on the other side of the room. When he entered he saw McCormick sitting in a chair next to Simone who was stripped down to her brazier while he wrapped a length of gauze around an oozing wound in her upper arm. The French detective sat quietly with her forehead cradled in the palm of her other hand as McCormick worked.

"How bad? Where's Maxine? You all right?" Clifford asked, stepping into the room.

"Just-a flesh wound, Chief. Max is upstairs, and I'm just dandy ... wish I could say as much for my living room," McCormick replied as he finished tying off the gauze strip.

"Yeah, it's a real mess out there. Better have a doctor look at that," Clifford said, coming over to Simone and putting a hand on her other shoulder. "You all right, detective?"

"*Oui, inspecteur*, I believe I will survive," she replied as she looked up at Clifford who noticed she was unusually white.

"You don't look so good," Clifford objected.

"Really, sir, I am, how you say, 'A-O-K'. It is just ... this is like your American Western movies, *comprendre*?"

"If ya mean we're like cowboys, yeah, I understand how ya feel," McCormick said as he stood up. "Look, you just sit there for a few minutes and rest, got it?"

"*Oui* ... got it," Simone replied ... That's when everyone heard the roar of the Thompson coming from upstairs.

"That's Mabel," Clifford barked.

"Maxine." McCormick added as both men bolted out the kitchen door.

"*Mon Dieu*, what is next," Simone moaned as she quickly and painfully put on her blouse, grabbed her gun lying on the table top, and followed the two men.

Clifford and McCormick ran up the stairs to the second floor where several uniforms, guns at the ready, were crouched in the hallway next to a bullet ridden bathroom door.

"We got one cornered, Chief," one of the officers reported.

"No you don't," McCormick replied dryly. "Maxine, fer cryin' out loud, it's just the cops. Don't shoot!" he yelled.

"Oh, sorry," they heard Maxine's voice say from behind the door. "Hey, can ya give a gal a hand, I think I'm stuck."

"Stand down, men," Clifford ordered as McCormick pushed past them and into the bathroom where Maxine sat on the toilet holding the smoking machine gun.

"Can ya believe it? I can't get up," she cursed.

McCormick stood there and laughed at her.

"Oh yeah, real funny, ya big lug. Now get over here and help me up," she snapped.

"Yes, dear," McCormick replied as he walked over to her. A second later, Clifford was behind him.

"Thanks for lending me Mable, Chief," Maxine said as she handed the weapon to McCormick, who then handed it to Clifford.

"No problem. Need-a hand?" Clifford replied.

"Yeah, looks like it," she sighed as McCormick put her arm around his neck and scooped her up.

"Gosh, I feel useless," Maxine said, as McCormick lifted her up.

"Yer kiddin' me right?" he said, kissing her mouth. Maxine touched his face and nodded. "And it looks like we need a new bathroom door too, huh?" he added.

"Oh, I'm sorry about that ... and those poor cops ..." Maxine apologized.

"Don't worry about it," Clifford said, coming over. "You okay, Maxine?"

"Yeah, we're fine. Thanks Chief," she yawned. "Mac, I'm sleepy ..."

"Say no more, cupcake," McCormick said as he swung her around and walked out of the room. "I'm putting her to bed, Chief, I'll be right back," he said over his shoulder as he walked down the hallway.

"Take yer time McCormick. All right boys, down stairs," he ordered the remaining cops. "I want an ambulance and the coroner here, pronto. Make it happen," he added.

"Yes, sir, Chief," the men responded.

Clifford turned around briefly as he heard the McCormick's bedroom door close farther down the hall. He looked down at the Thompson he held in his hand and shook his head. "I'm gettin' too old for this," he grumbled, and then he followed his men back down stairs.

Detective Simone Desaraux stood alone in the hallway just outside the parlor entrance staring down at the unknown assailant she had shot. His lifeless eyes stared back at her without emotion as she chewed on her bottom lip. After a few minutes she sighed heavily and looked at the Walther she held in her hand. That's when she heard a familiar voice behind her.

"First one?" Clifford asked gently.

Simone turned to him and simply nodded.

"The first one's always the toughest, detective."

"*Mon papa*, said that to me many years ago, when I became *un policier*. He prayed that I never have to take a life ... but now, here I am, in a foreign country, hunting the man who not only killed my father, but so many others, and now I question whether or not I am willing to do what I have to ..."

"All right look," Clifford interrupted, "you're a trained police officer. When the time comes you'll use your training to arrest this psycho you're after, or you'll do what you had to do here, defend yourself and your fellow officers. Now, if you can't do that, then you need to go back to France and let us handle this, otherwise pull yourself together and let's finish the job, got it?" Clifford rumbled and then he put a hand on top of her shoulder.

Simone sucked back some tears and nodded. "*Oui, Monsieur Chief*, I will not fail you," she replied.

"Good. Now, do you recognize any of these guys?" Clifford asked as he looked around.

"No, these men are strangers to me," she replied.

"Is there a chance any of these guys might be Canard?" McCormick asked as he approached the two.

"How's Maxine doing, detective?" Simone asked.

"Snoring like a boat motor," he replied.

"I have never seen anyone like your wife, she would make a formidable *gendarme*," Simone commended.

"A what?"

"Oh, forgive me ... a policeman," Simone translated.

McCormick and Clifford winked at each other and then changed the subject.

"Detective, is there a chance any of these dead men could be Andre Canard?" McCormick repeated.

"This is doubtful. These are hired ... how you say, 'thugs'."

"Well, maybe he's one of the others we captured trying to get away in that stolen van," Clifford said.

"What others?" Simone asked in surprise.

"The guys that took off and left their buddies behind, that's who. We were waiting for 'em down the street. We shot their tires out and captured five of 'em alive," Clifford replied.

"Any casualties?" McCormick asked.

"One tried to shoot his way out, but my men made short work of 'em," Clifford said. "Now, I propose we go downtown and see what these guys have to say. But first, we wait for the coroner to show up, then I'm putting a small army of cops in your place, Mac, just to make sure Maxine gets her beauty sleep … not that she needs it. In the meantime let's check the bodies for any information."

Simone and McCormick nodded in agreement and got to work.

Chapter Twelve

About an hour or so later, the rain was still falling heavily on the city when McCormick and Simone entered downtown police headquarters. They both shook off their respective umbrellas, and then walked through the crowded squad room towards Chief Clifford's office.

"Hi Mac. Hey, you guys okay? I heard there was some shooting at your house?" Fay said from behind her desk.

"We're all fine, Fay ... safe and sound for now. Is the Chief in there?" McCormick asked pointing with his thumb towards the office door.

"Nope, he's down in interrogation expecting you both. And if this crazy rain doesn't let up we're all gonna have to use a row boat to get home," Fay replied.

"Ya got that right, sister, I was plowing water in the streets to get here. Looks like the sewers are filling up fast too. Anyway, thanks, Fay, we'll head right down," McCormick said and turned to leave.

"By the way, daddy, how's Max and that baby doin'?" Fay grinned.

McCormick smiled back and gave her the thumbs up gesture. "They're good. I guess it won't be long."

"*Oui*, they are A-O-Kay," Simone added in broken English as she also held up her thumb.

Fay smiled humorously back at her and returned the gesture.

"Looks like we just might make an American outta you yet, detective. C'mon, let's go see what the Chief's caught," McCormick replied, taking Simone by the elbow and leading her away.

The interrogation rooms and cells were on the lower level of the building. McCormick and Simone stepped out of the elevator just in time to see Clifford exiting one of the rooms.

"Chief?" McCormick called.

Clifford turned towards them. "Good, you're both here. We need an interpreter; apparently these guys only speak French."

"I will speak with them," Simone said as she and McCormick came forward.

"In here," Clifford pointed with his thumb.

The three entered a room where an armed uniformed officer stood guard over a prisoner sitting in a chair with his hands cuffed behind his back. He was an unimpressive looking man wearing a black turtleneck sweater and sporting a goatee.

"Where's his pals?" McCormick asked.

"Cooling their heels in a holding cell under heavy guard. I picked this one out of the bunch at random. He had no wallet, no passport, no identification of any kind on 'em," Clifford replied.

The unidentified prisoner sat calmly and quietly as he looked the three over. Then he fixed his eyes on Simone and smiled.

"Vous êtes censé être mort," he said smugly.

"What'd he say?" Clifford asked.

"He says that I should be dead," Simone translated, and then she moved closer to the man and leaned forward. "*Vous serez bientôt* ... You, *monsieur*, soon will be when I take you back to France to be executed for your crimes," she replied in French. "Now, tell me, did Andre Canard send you? Tell me where he is and perhaps you will be spared the blade."

The prisoner merely laughed into her face. "Oh, you are much too beautiful a young woman to make such threats. Now, how about a kiss, huh?" he replied.

Simone stood straight up in shock.

"What'd he say?" Clifford asked. That's when Simone balled up a fist and struck the prisoner hard on the jaw, knocking him out of the chair and onto the concrete floor.

"Pig!" she spat, "tell me what I want to know. Where is Canard? *Où se trouve, Canard?*" she shouted.

"Whoa, take it easy," McCormick objected, taking her arm and pulling her away. "That's not how we do things around here," he cautioned.

"Detective, get outta here and cool off," Clifford reprimanded, and pointed at the door.

"*Je suis désolé* ... I am sorry. I am A-O-Kay ..."

"No, you're not A-OK. Now, go to the ladies room, splash your face, take a walk, cool off, and then get back here and conduct yourself professionally so we can get some information outta this mutt when he wakes up. That's an order, now get," Clifford barked.

Simone said something in French under her breath that sounded very unpleasant, but did what she was told and quickly left the room.

"Officer, get this guy off the floor and stick 'em back in that chair," Clifford ordered the cop standing nearby. The officer, with McCormick's assistance, got the prisoner up and maneuvered him into the chair. After a few minutes, he regained consciousness.

McCormick grabbed him by the front of his sweater and shook him fully awake.

"Welcome back, pal," McCormick said.

The Frenchman licked his bleeding lip and then laughed as he looked around the room, presumably for Simone.

"She'll be right back, and I suggest you mind your manners," McCormick warned.

The Frenchman looked up at McCormick and grinned.

"You ... You were one of them in the house, no?" he said in very broken English. "My only regret is not having shot that *putain* with the machine gun. Perhaps the next time we meet I will ..."

Before he could finish, McCormick hauled off and plowed him a hard, right cross, sending him back to the floor in a heap.

"Fer cryin' out loud, McCormick, what'd he say this time?" Clifford complained.

"I dunno the exact translation and I don't care. All I know is he threatened my wife," McCormick replied as he satisfactorily rubbed his knuckles.

Then Clifford turned to the cop in the room. "All right, officer, haul this guy outta here and put him in the cell with the others ... and then bring us another one that's still conscious," Clifford ordered.

"Yes, sir, Chief," the burly officer answered. Then he dragged the unconscious Frenchman out of the room by his feet.

"Well, we're not makin' any headway at this rate," Clifford growled.

"We got four or five more, right?" McCormick asked.

"Yeah."

"Well then, odds are one of 'em will talk," McCormick reasoned.

"Let's hope you're right. I'd hate to think your pretty house got shot up for nothin'. Looks like they wanted to get Simone pretty bad to send-a truck load of thugs to your place. Wonder what they'll try next?" Clifford said.

"Dunno, but whatever it is it won't be pleasant unless we can get one of these bozo's to spill they're guts," McCormick replied.

In the meantime, Simone stood in front the restroom mirror staring at herself. She wondered if she would have the courage to see this assignment through, if she would have to take any more lives in the line of duty. If, when the time came, she would have what it takes to bring down the man who murdered her father. She slowly shook her head in self-doubt, finally washing her hands as if they were covered in blood.

"*Que dirait votre père?* What would papa say?" she whispered to herself, as she wiped her hands dry on a provided towel. Afterward, she pinched the bridge of her nose, said a short prayer, and then left the restroom. When she returned to the interrogation room, she found a different prisoner sitting handcuffed in a chair.

"Feeling a little better, detective?" McCormick asked.

"*Oui, merci* ... but who is this, where is the other man?" she asked.

"He's back in his cell taking a nap," Clifford replied from another part of the room. "Now, detective, talk to this guy, find out if he speaks any English, if not, ask him about this Canard character."

"And this Red Hand gang," McCormick added.

"*Oui*, I will do my best," Simone replied as she approached the seated man.

He was a nervous looking younger man, somewhere in his early twenties and, like his comrades; he had no identification on him when captured. Simone quickly noticed the youthful prisoner's nervousness and was determined to capitalize on it.

"*Est-ce que vous parlez un peu anglais?* Do you speak any English?" she asked.

"No," the young man replied as he looked around the room at McCormick, Clifford, and the armed cop standing next to the door.

"*Regarde moi,* Look at me," she ordered, reaching out and pinching his face between her fingers, "*I* am the one you need to worry about, *comprenez vous? I* am the one who will take you back to France to face the noose, or the guillotine ... personally I prefer the guillotine over the rope, because I have seen so many youths like yourself not die instantly, but hang there and slowly strangle as there tongue turns black and ..."

"*Arrêtez ça,* Stop it," the young man objected as he jerked his face away from her hand. Now beads of perspiration began to appear on his forehead. Simone smiled inwardly and continued putting on the pressure.

"Are your parents alive? Your momma and your papa? What will they be thinking at your trial? What will they go through when their little boy is dragged from your prison cell to the block, eh?"

"*Arrêtez,* Stop, *madam,* what do you want from me?" the young man pleaded.

"Where is the man called Canard? Tell me now and perhaps I will ask *le juge* to be lenient?"

"I have heard that name mentioned by the others, but I have never seen him, I swear ... I only was recruited as a driver ... I drove *le van.* Please understand, I raced cars in Nice for money. We were poor, so poor, and so I helped some friends one day with a local robbery. I got away, but *mes amies*, my friends, were caught ... later I received a sum of money in an envelope under my door and then a telephone call asking me to be a driver, no questions asked. My parents needed the money, so I said, yes, and now here I am across the ocean driving for men with guns. They shot up a house looking for a French policeman ... I don't know why, they never told me?"

"*Petit ver* ... little worm, listen to me, *I* am the French policeman they seek for death, along with my American friends. Now, we are hunting this killer, Canard. Any information you can give us to assist in his arrest will go a long way towards how long you stay in prison or worse. We also need information or anything you know about *La Main Rouge*, the Red Hand gang that is here in America. So speak now. Do not waste my time or I will put you back into your cell with the others. This is your only opportunity, do not throw it away."

"*Madam*, I know nothing about this man you seek, I swear ..."

"It is *Détective* ... do not lie to me," Simone pressed.

"Please, I beg on my mother's life, I do not know this man, I have never seen him ... as for this Red Hand, I regret that I am now a part of it," the young man confessed and then began to weep. "I wish I had never accepted their money ... I wish ..."

"Enough," Simone replied, then she straightened up and informed the others in the room about the contents of the conversation. "What can we do for him as an incentive for his cooperation?" Simone asked.

Clifford rubbed his chin. "He's an illegal foreign national who engaged in criminal activity on American soil. He'll prolly be deported back to France."

"Chief, he's just-a kid," McCormick whispered, "and as far as we know, he hasn't fired a shot at anyone."

"Let me finish," Clifford replied. "If he cooperates, I won't put him back in the tank with his pals ... and maybe I can pull some strings and get the charges reduced... no promises though. Tell 'em he's got thirty seconds or the deals off."

"*Oui*, Chief," Simone nodded and then she explained the terms to the young man who seemed relieved, but still very much afraid.

"They will hunt me down," he began to say; "they told me that if I ever turned upon them they would kill me and my parents."

"We can offer you and your parents, protection, but you must cooperate now. What do you say?" Simone urged.

"What can I do? What choice do I have? I agree and God help me."

Simone turned to Clifford and nodded.

"Fine," Clifford said, then he ordered the other cop in the room to: "Uncuff him, get 'em some food and water, and then put him in a separate cell out of eyeshot of his pals. And I want an armed guard standing outside at all times, got that?"

"Yes, sir," the officer said as he unlocked the handcuffs and stood the young man up.

"You will be safe here," Simone told him, "arrange your thoughts, we will continue our conversation soon, understand?"

"*Oui, Détective ... merci,*" he replied, somewhat relieved. Then the officer took him away.

Chapter Thirteen

The brown haired, middle-aged, waitress had just finished her shift at the sleazy diner. She cursed quietly as she looked out a window at the downpour and wondered whether or not she should spend some of her meager tips on a taxi, or just hoof it to the room she rented several city blocks away. She looked into her purse and decided on the latter as she said a quick goodnight to the cook, and then ran out the swinging door onto the wet sidewalk. She was a block or so away when she felt something hard strike her on the back of the head, causing her to lose her vision for a moment. Then she felt a cord of some kind encircle her neck, and pull her into an alley she was passing by.

It was quick and almost painless ... she felt the breath leaving her body as she struggled against the stranger who had her in his grip ... soon her life of drudgery ebbed away ... and then finally ceased. She was lowered down onto the wet brickwork of the dirty alley; her arms folded across her chest, her right ear removed with almost surgical precision, and then she was left like so much trash, while the rain formed a puddle in silhouette around her.

Chief Clifford was notified from dispatch that a body had been found in an ally on the west side of town. Not an unusual occurrence, except for the method of death, and the disposition of the corps. Clifford took the elevator down to interrogation. When he arrived he walked over to one of the rooms that had a uniform standing outside the door, he knocked briefly, and then entered. In the center of the room stood a table with three chairs surrounding it occupied by McCormick, Simone, and the youthful prisoner who they had interrogated earlier the previous evening and whose name was Henri. Interrupted, the three looked at Clifford who motioned with his head for McCormick to step out. Once they were in the hallway, Clifford filled him in one the latest event.

"Sounds like our guy, doesn't it?"

"Yeah, sure does," Clifford replied. "How's it goin' with that kid?"

"He knows more than he thinks about the gang that recruited him ... and we have a location to check out. How do ya wanna proceed?"

"I want you and Desaraux to go and see about that body. Give me the address you got from the prisoner. I'll send a bunch of cops over there to see what we can scare out of the woodwork," Clifford said.

McCormick nodded and then went back into the room. A minute later he returned with Simone in tow, while the cop on duty was instructed to return the prisoner to his cell.

"And so it begins ... here," Simone said sadly.

"Let's not get ahead of ourselves. We won't be absolutely sure until we see the victim," McCormick answered.

"I gotta black and white for you to follow, McCormick. Let me know what you find, okay?" Clifford said as he walked away.

"You got it, Chief," McCormick answered, "Let's go," he said to Simone as the couple headed for the elevator.

By the time they arrived at the crime scene a small crowd had gathered despite the drizzle. The uniforms did their best to try to keep the gawkers and the members of the press away, as McCormick and Simone pushed past them and entered the ally where an assistant coroner was squatting next to the body, busy doing his job.

"Detectives McCormick and Desaraux, what ya got?" McCormick announced as he approached.

The coroner looked up and shook his head. "Well, it appears to be a case of a cruel robbery gone bad," he said, "blunt force trauma to the back of the skull and then death by strangulation, but I'll know more when I get her on the table. Then there's the missing ear, I don't get that?"

"*Mon Dieu,*" Simone sighed as she looked down at the dead woman.

"Robbery, huh? What'da ya make of the arms being folded over her chest?" McCormick asked.

"That is puzzling, I will have to admit," the coroner said as he stood up and stretched.

McCormick surveyed the ally, but didn't find what he was looking for until ...

"Detective," a cop interrupted, "we found this lying on the sidewalk," he said as he handed McCormick a woman's purse.

"Thanks, officer," McCormick replied, taking the purse and opening it up. "Let's see, lipstick, compact, some receipts and a wallet with ... let's see ...eight bucks and some change. Looks like robbery wasn't a motive after all," McCormick said looking over at the coroner.

The slightly embarrassed coroner nodded in agreement. "Well then as soon as you're finished here, detectives, I'll have a stretcher fetched," he replied, and then walked away.

McCormick and Simone knelt down to further examine the body.

"So, is it the same guy or not? What'da ya think?" McCormick asked Simone.

Simone examined the ligature marks on the throat, carefully turning the dead woman's head back and forth. Then she concentrated on the area where the victim's right ear should have been attached. "A very sharp blade was used to sever the ear just like the others back in France," Simone said quietly. As she examined the woman's hands, she noticed something ... a slip of folded paper sticking out of the coat sleeve, it was wedged under the wrist watch.

"*Qu'est-ce que c'est?* What is this?" she said as she carefully removed the paper.

"What ya got?" McCormick asked.

"I do not know," Simone said as she took the paper and opened it. It was a note written in French.

"What is it?" McCormick asked again.

Simone put a hand to her mouth as she read and then she handed it to McCormick.

"What's it say?" he asked.

"It is addressed to me," Simone replied, visibly shaken. "It says: 'There will be others, and that *I* will be like this woman soon'. *Mon Dieu*, what have we unleashed upon this city?"

"He's trying to scare you, get you off balance. Don't worry, we'll get him," McCormick said, taking the note and putting it into an inside jacket pocket. "Well, at least we know now that this is our guy and not some random crackpot," he said as he stood and then helped Simone to her feet. Afterward, he signaled for the stretcher to be brought over. The body was covered, and the personal effects of the deceased were given to a uniform. "Make sure next of kin are informed, will ya?" he instructed the cop.

"You got it. Okay, folks, make some room," the officer announced to the crowd that was inching closer.

"Hey, Detective, is this the work of a mass murderer?" someone yelled, no doubt a reporter.

"No comment. And you need to keep yer trap shut. This is an ongoing investigation," McCormick answered bluntly. "C'mon," he said taking Simone by the arm, "let's get outta here."

Simone Desaraux

The two walked quickly to McCormick's car, got in, and pulled away from the curb. Little did they realize that someone in the crowd was watching them with great interest. He was a tall, well-built man, wearing a trench coat and hat with the brim pulled down low. He waited until the car was out of sight before he crossed the street and got into the passenger's side of a waiting gray sedan. Once he had shut the door the driver offered him a cigarette.

"*Merci*," the passenger replied as the driver conveniently struck a stick match and lit the end of the cigarette.

"*Quel est votre souhait?*" the French driver asked as he extinguished the match and shoved it out the side window which was opened a crack.

"What is my wish?" the passenger replied with annoyance, "my wish is to find the idiots who have mishandled the raid on that *détective's* home. The Desaraux woman and the other female were supposed to be captured and any others killed. I was assured that we had reliable men in the Red Hand, am I mistaken?"

"It appears there are inconsistencies in the ranks," the driver apologized.

"We should have sent you, Pierre, you have never failed me yet," the passenger replied, putting his hand briefly on the drivers arm.

"*Merci, monsieur*, I appreciate the *confiance* you have placed in me," Pierre replied, respectfully. "However, if I may be so bold ... we should inform *him* of current events. He will not be pleased, I'm sure."

The passenger took a long drag on the imported cigarette, and then crushed it out in the palm of his leather gloved hand. "This was supposed to be a simple transition," he muttered angrily, more to himself than to the driver. "There are millions of francs at stake. If this does not begin to go our way, there will be the devil to pay."

"*Oui, monsieur*, I fear you are correct. However, there is still time for us to conclude our business here, provided *la police* can be distracted long enough," Pierre replied cautiously.

The passenger sat quietly for a few minutes, watching the crowd across the street disperse from the crime scene. The driver also watched as patrol cars pulled away, along with the coroners van.

"You do not agree with my little distractions, do you Pierre?" the passenger quietly asked.

Pierre cleared his throat before carefully answering. "Sir, it is not my place to say. This is not why I have been attached to you for so long. We all have our individual plagues to deal with. My responsibility is to assist and protect, not to judge you."

The passenger turned and smiled thinly at the driver. "Well said ... I appreciate your honesty."

"*Merci*, then forgive my boldness if I recommend that perhaps you might control your urges until our business here is concluded. Afterward, this city and its streets are yours," Pierre cautiously advised.

"My hunger is quenched for the time being," the passenger replied. "However, the Desaraux woman must be dealt with, and soon ... she is mine, do you understand?"

"*Oui, monsieur*, I understand completely ... and she will be. Once the affair we have been hired for is successfully concluded, you can take your time with her," Pierre said.

The passenger grinned and nodded, like he had just tasted something sweet. Then he motioned for Pierre to drive away.

As they drove, the passenger asked. "Pierre, explain to me why this other woman is *nécessaire*, necessary. I do not understand how she fits in with any of our plans ... and I understand that she is *enceinte*, pregnant?"

"*Oui*, that is also my understanding. All I know is that *he* wants her alive and unharmed. Those were the instructions."

"More complications I fear," the passenger mused out loud. "Perhaps, you are correct, Pierre ... perhaps it is time I make a *téléphone* call to *Monsieur* Smith."

Chapter Fourteen

"What'da ya mean yoo found nothin'?" Sal Canale said from behind his desk.

"I'm tellin' ya, Sal, this guy we killed at the restaurant's a ghost," the hood called Vinnie replied as he stood next to another man in front of Sal's desk.

"Hey, that's a good one Vin, 'the guy's a ghost' after he got shot, get it?" he chuckled stupidly.

"Shut your face, Luigi, will ya?" Vinnie barked, looking over at him.

"Knock it off you two," Sal reprimanded. "Vinnie, what'da ya talkin' about?"

"I'm sayin' that dead hit man's got no past here, or anywhere ... I mean nothin'. It's like he just appeared outta nowhere, and nobody in this town knows nothin' about him either."

"Or they just ain't talkin' ... this disturbs me," Sal interrupted, leaning forward and putting his hands on the desk top. "Somebody put a hit on that French dame in *our* place of business and in *our* town. This we can't tolerate," he emphasized while tapping with a finger. "What about this Red Hand gang that's movin' in, anything?"

Both men standing before Sal shook their heads. Then Luigi spoke up ...

"Hey, maybe this gang's just a figmentation of somebodies imagination, huh? What'da yas think?"

Sal lowered his head into both hands and moaned, "Aye yigh yigh."

"Sorry, Sal," Vinnie apologized on behalf of his partner. "Luigi, take-a hike, will ya? I'll be right out," Vinnie ordered as he pointed towards the door.

"Okay, Vin, see ya." Luigi left the office, closing the door behind him.

"Where'd ya find that mook, Sal?" Vinnie asked, pointing with his thumb behind him.

"Don't ask, Vin. All I know is that we're somehow related, and I'm supposed to be doin' somebody a favor, *capire*?"

"Yeah, I get it ... Where's Louie been anyway?"

"Here's on his way back from a-job. When he gets here, I want yoos two guys to turn this town upside down. I want ya's to shake down anybody that you think knows anything about anything with regard to this Red Hand gang, even if yas have to break some knee caps, understand?"

"Yeah, Sal, I got it."

"If these French mooks think they can just waltz into my town and start shootin', they got another thing comin'. Now, beat it. And check on Nicky before you leave, will ya?"

"Okay, Sal," Vinnie said and then he turned and left.

Sal leaned back in his plush leather chair and rubbed the side of his face with the back of his hairy hand in contemplation. After a few long minutes, a thought suddenly occurred to him that made him feel very uncomfortable. "I wonder ..." he whispered out loud, and then he picked up the telephone and dialed.

In the meantime, another telephone call was being made from a backroom of a storage facility near the docks. The Frenchman sat behind an old desk with the receiver pressed to his ear while he smoked, waiting for the ringing on the other end of the line to turn into ...

"Hello?"

"*Bonjour*, I wish to speak with *Monsieur Smith, s'il vous plait*," he answered in broken English.

"Whom shall I say is calling?"

"Tell him it is, Andre Canard."

"One moment, please ..."

The Frenchman waited and smoked. He was becoming impatient and about to hang up when ...

"Well, well, its Monsieur Canard now is it?" a deep and booming British voice said on the other end of the line. "I must confess I find myself more enamored by some of your other aliases rather than Canard."

"This one will suffice for the time being, *Monsieur Smith*," Canard replied, as he crushed out his cigarette into an ashtray.

"I see. Now, I suspect you have a good reason for making a telephone call to me at this unsuitable hour?"

"*Oui. Monsieur Smith*, while I appreciate your support in our business transaction, I fail to understand why you send me *incompétent* people for such a large task?"

"Yes, yes, I have been informed of the regrettable outcome of the assault on the McCormick house, and also the botched attempt at the restaurant. Rest assured though, and despite these setbacks, all things are proceeding as planned."

"I also fail to understand how the pregnant wife of a local private *détective* is pertinent to our business?"

"And I understand and appreciate your concern, sir," Smith answered abruptly. "However, the disposition of Mrs. McCormick in these matters is of very personal interest to me and I will have my way, make no mistake. Had the intervention at the McCormick home gone correctly we would not be having this conversation, I'm sure. Nevertheless, we must take into consideration all factors at this time. I would ask you to follow my instructions to the letter and without question from this time forward. Doing so will assure our eventual success at the end of our venture along with our mutual enrichment. Do we agree, Monsieur Canard?

Canard tightened his jaw momentarily. He hated the thought of being under the thumb of someone he had never met, especially one that was so 'British'.

"*Oui*, of course, *monsieur*. It is just these recent events are making matters more *compliqué* ... what is word?"

"Complicated, I believe is the word you are searching for, sir," Smith chuckled.

"*Oui.* This McCormick *détective* and the Desaraux woman will, I fear, interfere with our plans."

"So kill her my good man. Isn't that what you do for, shall we say, a hobby?"

Canard took a deep breath as he held his anger in check. "She is surrounded now by the police because of the failure at the restaurant."

"May I remind you, *monsieur*, that you hired a local gangster to handle this without my knowledge or consent. The failure is entirely on your shoulders, sir, so handle it," Smith scolded.

"And I shall, but apparently, I suspect that you are unaware that this fool of a local gangster did not use one of his own people … he used one of yours," Canard responded acidly.

There was strained silence for a few moments, until …

"Oh, my … that is regrettable news, I must say," Smith replied soberly. "Thank you for informing me of this infraction of protocol. This does change matters somewhat."

"How is that?"

Well, knowing how clever and resourceful Detective McCormick and his associates can be, and based on my considerable experience with him, I suspect it will not be long before he understands the nature of the parties involved in our very personal business ... dear, dear. Monsieur, Canard, would you please give me a few minutes to confer? I will be back shortly ..."

"Of course," Canard replied and then he took out another cigarette and waited. Two more cigarettes later, Smith returned.

"There now. I apologize for the inconvenience," Smith began, "you will be pleased to know that our business will continue as agreed by all parties. The products, I have been assured, will arrive on schedule. I have arranged adequate accommodations for them ... and of course, you know your part. Now, as to this other matter we've discussed, we would like you to handle a few tasks on your end. Let me explain ..."

Chapter Fifteen

The end of the next day found McCormick and Simone no further along in their investigation than they were the day before.

"The boy, Henri, has told us all that he knows, I'm sure of it," Simone said as she sat sipping a cup of coffee in Chief Clifford's office."

"Yeah, I tend to agree. There's nothin' more he can help us with, and those other guys ain't talkin' either by the looks of it," McCormick said, crossing his legs as he sat in a chair next to her.

"That address the kid gave us was a dead end too. It was all cleaned out by the time we got there, they even swept the floor ... no evidence period, blast it," Clifford growled, and then buried his face in his coffee mug.

"There is one thing though," McCormick offered.

"Yeah, what's that?" Clifford asked.

"I gotta interesting phone call from Sal Canale."

"Oh yeah? I hope its good news, I could use some," Clifford replied.

"He's been pretty helpful so far," McCormick said.

"*Oui*, I very much appreciated his *hospitalité*," Simone added.

"Yeah, yeah, great, so what'd he have to say?" Clifford asked.

"He had a hunch and I think it might be worth checkin' out," McCormick replied.

"A hunch about what?"

"*Excuse moi*? A hunch?" Simone asked.

"Yeah, you know, we talked about that your first day here, remember?" McCormick said.

Oh, *oui*, you mean *une intuition*?"

"Yeah, whatever you said. Anyway, Sal's idea is that there's something bigger goin' on around here than just a killer and his gang movin' into town."

"Like what?" Clifford asked.

Suddenly, Fay burst into the office.

"Chief, something's happened, something bad," she announced urgently.

"Slow down, Fay, what's goin' on?" Clifford said, standing up.

"It's down in interrogation ... its bad Chief ..."

"All right. Fay, you stay here. McCormick, Detective, come with me," Clifford ordered as he grabbed his suit jacket off the back of his chair and stormed out the office door with the other two close behind him. When the elevator doors slid opened, the basement hallway was lined with cops with drawn weapons.

"All right, report," Clifford bellowed as he exited.

"Down here, boss," a portly sergeant motioned. Clifford and the others pushed their way through the maze of uniforms and down to where the jail cells were located. When they entered the room they all stopped abruptly.

"*Mon Dieu,*" Simone gasped, putting a hand over her mouth.

"This is how the morning shift found 'em, Chief," the cop said quietly.

Four unmoving bodies lay on the stone floor of the jail cell. Another, the on-duty night watch officer, lay slumped against a wall with a neat round hole in his forehead.

"Henri?" Simone said fearfully.

"Down here," the sergeant directed.

The four now walked out of the room via another exit, down a hallway, and into another block of cells used for solitary confinement. The young prisoner, Henri, was found sitting on his bunk with his head against the concrete wall, staring up at the ceiling. His mouth was open, and his eyes fixed.

"*Oh, Henri, qu'ont-ils fait pour vous*? What have they done to you," Simone sighed in despair.

"How the blazes did this happen?" Clifford shouted at the officer.

"I dunno, boss," the red-faced sergeant answered.

"You don't know?" Clifford bellowed. "I'll tell ya what I know. I want this entire building locked down tight, understand? Nobody leaves, nobody comes in, got it? Now move," Clifford ordered. The officer nodded and quickly left.

Simone approached the open cell door and entered the enclosure. She looked down at the young man, placed a hand against his cheek, said a brief prayer, and then began to examine him.

"What'da ya got?" McCormick asked as he stood behind her.

"He has been strangled. His neck is broken ... but there is something else," she said as she continued her examination.

"What?" McCormick asked, leaning forward.

"Look at his lips," she pointed out with an index finger.

McCormick looked more closely and noticed that the young man's lips were slightly blue.

"What'da ya got?" Clifford asked as he also entered the cell.

"Take-a look at this Chief?" McCormick invited.

Clifford came forward and leaned in next to Simone who showed Clifford the boy's mouth.

"Poison?" Clifford asked.

"*Oui*, I believe so ... or something similar."

Clifford stood up. "Well, if he was poisoned, why strangle him?"

"I gotta hunch. Let's take-a look at the others," McCormick suggested.

Before leaving the cell, Simone carefully closed the young man's eyes, and then followed the two men back to the main block of holding cells where several cops stood.

Clifford reached for the cell door and pulled, but it was locked.

"Keys!" he barked.

Once of the cops came running with the cell keys and let the trio inside. Four bodies lay, as if frozen in time, in various positions in the cell. Some on the floor, while others on top of bunks. Simone went over to check on the nearest corpse when McCormick ordered her to ...

"Stop! Don't touch anything."

Simone looked at him with surprise, but did as she was told.

"Chief, I need medical gloves for this," McCormick asked.

"You heard the man, go fetch some gloves and get the coroner down here a.s.a.p.," Clifford ordered his men.

A few minutes later, McCormick was sliding on a pair of rubber gloves over his large hands.

"What're ya thinkin', Mac?" Clifford asked.

"I'm thinkin' I've seen this before … years ago at some guy's pawn shop, remember?"

Clifford scratched the white stubble on his face and then his eyes widened. "Yer kidd'n me, right?"

"Let's hope I'm wrong," McCormick replied as he went to the nearest body lying face down and attempted to turn him over. "This guy's like stone," McCormick said as he struggled to maneuver him. When he got him onto his back, everyone noticed the expression of terror on the dead man's face and his hands clutched around his throat as if he were choking. McCormick turned and spit before he stood up, and then he briefly examined the other bodies.

"Well?" Clifford asked

"All the same, hard as a rock and as dead as," McCormick replied.

"Please, I do not understand what is happening?" Simone asked, feeling left out.

"I'll explain later, detective, but for right now, don't touch anything in here. In fact, go and scrub your hands good after touching that kid," McCormick advised as he held his hands away from his body. Simone headed at a quick walk to the nearest lavatory.

"So, Mac, you think it's them?"

McCormick worked his jaw and then looked directly at Clifford. "I know it's them, Chief. This stinks of them."

Clifford pushed the hat back on his head, rubbed his forehead, and cursed freely.

"This is just what we need, blast it," he muttered angrily. "Hey, how come the kid isn't in the same shape as these others?"

McCormick stood very still for a few moments contemplating what Clifford had observed. And then he said: "Well, my theory is whoever did this figured out the kid was spilling his guts to us. I think they interrogated him to find out what he told us, and then they took care of him."

"Makes sense, if we're dealin' with who we think we are. Looks like the others were expendable," Clifford said.

McCormick nodded, "These other guys were older, seasoned, they weren't gonna talk, not right away anyway. But I imagine their bosses didn't want any loose ends ..."

There was a commotion behind them now as an assistant coroner, and his assistant, arrived with some medical personnel carrying stretchers.

"What's going on here, Chief Clifford? I was right in the middle of an autopsy when I was interrupted by ... Oh, my, what's happened down here?" he said as he now saw the bodies.

"This is a crime scene, that's what, and a black eye for the department," Clifford growled. "Now, these men have been exposed to an unknown substance, so take extra precautions and wear gloves, got it? I don't want any more fatalities today,"

"Well, if that's the case shouldn't we call the CDC if there is a contagion here? In fact we should probably quarantine the entire building and ..."

"That won't be necessary, doc. As far as I know the stuff used on these men is not widely contagious, like the measles or somethin', but it could be on their clothes, so be careful," McCormick advised.

"And you are, who? Are you in the medical field?" the coroner sarcastically asked.

"No, I'm in the field of personal experience," McCormick retorted.

"All right, listen up, doc," Clifford barked, "you just do what you're told and keep your trap shut about this. I don't want a city-wide panic. We're treating this as an execution, not an epidemic. Now, quit flappin' your yap and do your job, pronto."

The chastised coroner reluctantly nodded, donned a pair of rubber gloves, and then went into the cell with his assistant.

"And I want a full report, yesterday ... blood work, the whole nine yards. This is your top priority, got it?" Clifford demanded.

"Yes, Chief," the assistant replied, snapping his own gloves onto his hands.

"And by the way, there's another one in solitary ... a kid, treat him with respect," Clifford added.

The two medical men turned, looked at Clifford, nodded, and got to work.

"*Merci*," Simone said quietly as she returned.

Clifford reached out and squeezed her unwounded arm. "Thank me at the end of the day if we're all still alive. Now, there's nothing more you two can do down here. So, why don't you both go upstairs and brief Fay, and tell her no one is to breathe a word about what's happened down here. If the press gets wind of this there'll be hell to pay, understand?"

"Got it, boss," McCormick said. Then he turned to the assistant medical. "Hey, pal, you got a way to dispose of these?" he asked, holding out both rubber gloved hands.

"Yeah, sure, hang on," the man said as he left the cell and returned with a heavy canvas bag. He opened one end and set it upright on the floor. "Let's see them hands."

McCormick held out both hands to the assistant, and he yanked the rubber gloves off, inside out, and deposited them into the sturdy sack. After snapping the top closed he gave McCormick the thumbs up.

"Check for any kind of white powder on them gloves, will ya? Let us know what you find," McCormick said quietly.

"All right. Anything else?"

"Nope, just be careful. Detective, let's get outta here," he said to Simone. Then they both walked out of the room.

Chapter Sixteen

"Are yoos kiddin' me, McCormick? Somebody put-a hit on the police station? Sal Canale said into the telephone receiver.

"Yeah, and keep it under your hat, will ya? We don't want the press to get wind of it," McCormick replied.

"Hey, mum's the word ... no worries. So, who died?"

"Every one of the guys we had in custody that hit my house. It was like you said when you called earlier ... it's them," McCormick said.

"Yeah, I kinda had'a hunch it just might be. So, what'da we gonna do about it?"

"I dunno. We're dead in the water right now. We got zip for evidence on how to find 'em ... *and* a killer on the loose. I can't wait to see what happens next," McCormick replied.

Three heavily loaded tractor trailer trucks pulled slowly into a cavernous warehouse near the docks a little after midnight as the heavy fog rolled in off the bay. The trucks all lined up next to each other, and then shut down their engines. A huge overhead door behind them ponderously lowered, plunging the interior into pitch blackness, except for the three sets of headlights still burning in the trucks. The drivers got out, went to the front of their respective rigs, and stood there silently in the headlight beams. After a few minutes, three other men approached from out of the blackness and stopped before each of the drivers.

"Any problems?" the driver in the middle was asked by a rough-voiced man.

The driver merely shook his head.

"Okay, leave the rigs here, follow us to get your dough, and then disappear. Keep yer traps shut and maybe there'll be more work later."

The drivers nodded in compliance, and then all three followed another man away, leaving two behind.

"C'mon, let's check the order," the rough-voiced man directed.

The two walked to the rear of the first truck where a master key appeared in one of the men's hand. "Where's your flashlight?" he asked the other.

Once the rear of the truck was illuminated, the padlock was removed, the handle securing the double doors was unlatched, and then one of the doors was swung to one side revealing the interior that was filled to the roof with ....

"Looks like everything's here," the rough-voiced man said as he played the flashlight beam over the outside of the tightly packed cargo.

"What'da they need all this stuff for, huh?" the other man asked.

"We ain't gettin' paid to asked questions," the rough-voiced man replied with irritation as he handed the light back to his partner, and then shut and relocked the trailer door.

The same inspection was made on the two remaining trucks, except for one small difference. When the door was swung open on the last trailer the flashlight beam illuminated something out of place ... a dead body lying on the floor.

"What the?"

"Never mind, just pull him outta there," the rough-voiced man ordered.

The other man did as he was told. A moment later the sound of a heavy corpse thudded on the concrete floor.

"Okay, listen up," the rough-voice man began, "go gett'a gunny sack and a dolly. Then you and one of the other men take this stiff and throw him in the bay. Make sure you put some weight in the bottom of the sack so he'll sink, got it? I'll take care of this here. Now move."

"Yeah, sure," the other man reluctantly replied.

"... and leave the flashlight."

The other man slowly shook his head, gave back the flashlight, and then trotted off into the blackness.

When he was gone the rough-voiced man played the light over the corpse. Then he knelt down for a closer look. It was the body of a man dressed in a long, heavy overcoat. When the coat was unbuttoned and opened, it revealed a uniform, along with a holster without a weapon. Decorating the front of the uniform, just above the breast pocket, was a badge indicating that the man was a Canadian Border Patrol officer, and just to the left of that was a bullet hole.

"Guess you was snoopin' around the wrong cargo, huh?" the ruff-voiced man commented nonchalantly as he took the badge off the uniform, stood up, and then pointed the light back into the still open trailer. Like the others that had been examined, the cargo of boxes, emblazoned with a red cross, was stacked floor to ceiling with medical supplies. "Hmm, looks like somebody's expectin' a war," the man grunted. Then he closed and secured the trailer.

Meanwhile, two prisoners met in the exercise yard of Alcatraz prison. The men looked about to see where the armed guards were stationed around them, then they casually walked over to an isolated spot along the high stone wall.

Manie Stracuzzi leaned against the wall, took out a smoke, and then offered one to the other man. After a shared match was lit the two men smoked as if passing the time. When they both were sure they were not being watched, Manie spoke.

"So, what ya got for me, huh?"

"Plenty," the other prisoner replied as he nervously looked around the yard at the other prisoners milling about, "and it's gonna cost ya. This ain't free."

"Yeah, yeah, I hear yas ... and I'm good for whatever it is you think you want ... 'cept of course a ticket outta this joint," Manie grimly joked.

The other man spit a piece of tobacco out of his mouth before taking another drag on his Camel.

"You'd better be. Welchers don't last long here ..."

"Hey, I been here awhile, so don't get nervous," Manie responded. "Now, let's have it before the screws break us up."

"Okay, so I already told ya last time about the Red Hand gang settin' up shop ..."

"Yeah, yeah, and you said they was hauling cargo through town. What's the cargo?"

The other man leaned in. "I hear its medical supplies."

"Huh? Yer kiddin' ... medical supplies? What for?" Manie asked.

"Don't know that ... yet, but, there's a lot of it ... comin' down from Canada, like I told yas before."

"Uh-huh. Okay, where they located?"

"Oh, so you want an address do ya?"

"Yeah, that would be nice ... now spill it," Manie threatened.

"Take it easy ... Warehouse district, east-side docks, that's all I know. Look, we both could get our throats cut for even talkin' about this ..."

"Yeah, okay. Now, what about this lunatic that's goin' around creatin' corpses?"

"All I know is he's French, and he's a ghost. Just like we're gonna be if I keep pokin' my nose around for ya. This is the last time, by the way," the other prisoner said as he nervously took out one of his own cigarettes and lit it.

"Do ya think he's in with the Red Hand gang?" Manie asked, but before the other prisoner could answer ...

"All right you two, break it up. Walk off," a burly guard commanded as he held his rifle.

The two prisoners didn't reply, but just walked away from each other and into the crowd of other inmates.

Several hours later, Manie Stracuzzi sat on his bunk in his cell reading an out of date newspaper, when all of a sudden the alarm went off in the cell block.

"What's goin' on?" Manie said, putting the paper down next to him.

"Dunno," his cellmate replied, "maybe it's a break?"

"Fat chance of that," Manie replied as he looked out between the bars at guards running by. A few minutes later, one of the guards stopped in front of the cell door and spoke, "Thought you'd wanna know, Stracuzzi, your friend is dead."

Manie looked surprised. "My friend? What friend?"

"Prisoner 76550 ... you know, the guy you was yakin' to in the yard this mornin' ... Johnny Mills ... you two was pal's, right?"

Manie immediately wiped the sweat that suddenly appeared on his upper lip.

"Nah, no, we wasn't friends ... just talkin', is all," Manie replied to the guard.

"Yeah, well, your friend won't be doin' any more talkin' ... somebody shived 'em good. Just thought you'd wanna know. We're on lock down, so supper's gonna be late," the guard added, and then he walked away.

Manie just sat there looking at his hands.

"Tough break for your pal," Manie's cellmate casually said as he stood up and walked over to the cell door.

"Like I told that screw, we wasn't pals ... just-a guy I was talkin' to this mornin'," Manie replied.

"Yeah, just-a guy," the other prisoner repeated as he looked both ways down the catwalk running by the bloc of cells. Then he slowly turned around, and as he did a loop of thin rope appeared in his hand. "Ya gotta big nose, a big mouth, and cop friends, Stracuzzi. Ya should'a minded your own business. The Red Hand don't like informants ..."

"Huh? Whaa …" Manie blurted as the man rushed upon him and expertly twisted the rope around his neck.

"Say goodnight, ya rat," the other prisoner whispered as Manie Stracuzzi breathed his last.

Simone Desaraux

Chapter Seventeen

Gottfried Smith casually wandered down the plush, carpeted hallway, smoking a Havana cigar as he admired the row of paintings hanging along the walls. He would stop his ponderous waddle ever so often to muse at original oils by Monet, Vermeer, and Raphael. He smiled to himself as he studied the works, inserting the Cuban into his wide mouth and sucking in the smoke, which he held for a satisfying moment in his lungs, and then vented into the air.

He continued on down the hall, smoking and admiring, when his sojourn was interrupted by a tiny throat being cleared from behind him.

"Excuse me, sir, but your guest has arrived. She is waiting in the parlor as you requested," the young, pretty maid announced.

Smith turned half-way around and nodded at her, and at the same time dismissing her. She understood the silent cue, curtsied, and then quickly left.

Smith turned back towards the wall of priceless artwork and smiled at this collection, one of many collections he possessed, hanging in many different mansions around the world. When he felt sufficiently satiated, he turned his great body towards the exit, shoving the half-smoked cigar into his mouth. He slid his chubby hands into his imported, tailored suit trouser pockets, as he slowly walked to meet his announced house guest.

The athletic looking oriental woman sat quietly with her eyes closed upon a Toscano high back leather sofa. She wore a simple black silk jumpsuit, no jewelry, except for the ornate comb which held a twisted bun of voluptuous raven black hair behind her head.

When Smith entered the room, she didn't move a muscle, nor did she open her eyes. However, a slight smile did form on her lips as Smith crossed the room, attempting to be as stealthy as an elephant-sized man could be.

"You're smoking Cubans again, Mr. Smith," she announced casually with perfect English diction, "and you have new shoes ... Italian I believe. Am I wrong?"

Smith chuckled with amusement as he approached the woman from behind. He stopped briefly to look at the back of her head, then he came around to the front of the sofa, and stood before her like a great mountain.

"I see you haven't lost your talent for details, my dear Miss Sato," Smith complimented, "and congratulations on the completion of your assignment in Japan. I have been informed that because of its success we can continue with our project without hindrance."

Yumi Sato opened her almond shaped eyes and then managed to part her lips, ever so quickly, in what would amount to a vague acknowledgement of her host's approval. She never smiled openly, nor laughed. Those emotions simply were not present in her nature, or in the nature of her work. She quickly rose from the sofa, catlike in her movements. The woman was tall, much taller than would be expected for a female of her race, her dark eyes taking in everything all at once.

"Are we alone?" she asked, quickly scanning the room and then staring at Smith.

"Indeed, my dear, quite alone … and the house is secure, I assure you.

"Good," she acknowledged, as she extended her right hand to Smith who took it up and respectfully kissed the back of it. It was then that Smith noticed something.

"Your hand is bruised," Smith said, as he examined it.

The woman snatched it back from him and rubbed the knuckles.

"It's nothing to concern yourself with, Mr. Smith; I heal quickly and besides ..."

"Besides what? Smith replied.

Sato turned and walked a few paces away, and then turned around to face Smith again.

"You should see the other guy," she replied.

Smith rumbled with laughter as he tipped his head with respect in her direction, and then took a drag on his cigar. Sato just stood and watched without amusement.

"May I offer you some refreshment?" Smith asked, walking over to a table in the room that held a variety of wines and liquor.

"None for me, thank you. One must be, shall we say, always on the alert," she replied.

"Indeed, and I respect that, Miss Sato. However, if you don't mind, I will indulge myself," Smith said, as he mixed a martini. "Now then, tell me the details of your visit to your home country, if you would," Smith said turning away from the table.

"Actually, my home country is New York City. My mother was Japanese. As for my father, I never knew him."

"I see. Well, then, to business," Smith replied.

Sato, placed both hands behind her back and began to pace mechanically, back and forth, in front of Smith as she dictated, almost machine-like, the events of the last seventy-two hours of her assignment overseas.

Smith listened carefully as the woman related, in great detail, what he needed to hear. When she was finished, she stood almost at attention, and then bowed deeply at the waist. Smith put down his drink, and his cigar, and applauded loudly.

"Well done, Miss Sato, you have exceeded my expectations," he said. "I must say, if you continue to have as much success in the future, you will certainly rival the late, Madam Zhenobia."

Sato, straightened up and nodded a salute. "Thank you. I regret that I never had the opportunity to meet her in person, she is regarded as a legend among us."

"Indeed," Smith replied somberly, "a great loss to the organization. However, progress does not dwell upon the past. We must move forward into this new decade that is upon us and make it ours. Now, we have a local situation that needs your expertise.

Chapter Eighteen

McCormick's police car radio sounded off as Chief Clifford's voice boom through the speaker causing it to rattle noisily.

"Mac? You there? I got news," Clifford anxiously announced.

McCormick, along with Simone, had just pulled away from the crime scene and were heading for downtown. McCormick picked up the microphone and replied.

"Right here, Chief. What's the good word?"

"Plenty, you and Detective Desaraux get yourselves to the docks, pronto. I'll meet you there with reinforcements," Clifford replied back.

"The docks? Reinforcements? What's going on down there, another body?"

"Mon Dieu, not another ..." Simone sighed.

"Hang on sister," McCormick cautioned, "Chief, what's goin' on at the docks?"

"Never mind, this is an open channel. I'll tell ya when you get there, just step on it. Clifford out."

"Sounds serious, guess we'd better hurry," McCormick said to Simone as he stepped down hard on the accelerator. The Caddy lunged forward, causing Simone to cling tenaciously to her purse and the dashboard.

They arrived at the warehouse district in short order and parked behind a line of patrol cars. They both got out and began to walk, not really knowing where they were going, when they heard someone whistle. It was Chief Clifford in the distance waving his arms at them. The couple dog-trotted to where Clifford stood, next to one of the massive brick warehouses that lined the pier.

"What's goin' on Chief?" McCormick puffed as he and Simone came to a halt.

"We gotta hot tip from our friend Sal, that's what. It seems that Manie Stracuzzi character we visited the other day in Alcatraz, and who by the way was just found dead in his cell, managed to get a message out before he checked out. Sal says the Red Hand gang is using this warehouse to move supplies for some project they got goin' on. We're just about to raid the place. Thought you, and the detective here, might wanna join the party."

"Gotta warrant?" McCormick asked, skeptically.

Clifford smiled around his toothpick as he reached into his suit coat pocket and pulled out a folded, official looking paper.

"Yep, all legal. Happy now? Okay, let's go."

Clifford turned to the dozen or so heavily armed policemen with their backs pressed against the wall of the building, and gave them the go ahead signal. The next thing that was heard was the sound of glass being broken, as high windows along the wall were smashed and cops were boosted by fellow officers up through the openings. A few minutes later the massive overhead door ascended allowing the rest of the cops to pour into the building. Clifford, McCormick, and Simone entered behind the crush of blue uniforms as every inch of the interior was searched.

"Nothing, blast it," Clifford cursed as he angrily threw away his tooth pick.

"It was a long shot anyway, Chief," McCormick replied as he looked around the empty interior of the place. Simone also made a full turn around, hoping to find something, but shook her head in disappointment. Suddenly, they heard shouting from the other side of the place as several police officers waved frantically at the three.

"Over here!" they shouted. McCormick and Simone broke into a dead run, while Clifford, groaning with inconvenience, followed at a quick walk.

When McCormick and Simone got to the other side of the building, the cops hurried them through a back door which emptied out onto the docks. They noticed a group of officers at the edge of the dock, looking and pointing at something below them in the water. McCormick, with Simone at his heels, hurried over and peeked over the edge. They now both saw what the commotion was about … a dead man floating half-in, half-out, of the swirling water surrounding the pylons.

"Mon Dieu," Simone commented as she observed the bobbing corpse.

When Clifford arrived, he bent in half, grabbing his knees and trying to catch his breath. "What'ta we got?" he puffed. McCormick pointed at the body. Clifford nodded his head and straightened up, "Alright, what's everyone standin' around gawkin' at? Get that guy outta the drink, pronto," he ordered. A little while later, the dead man was being hauled up onto the dock along with a canvas bag that was wrapped around his legs.

"Get the coroner down here, and I want this entire place locked down, got it?" Clifford ordered his men. Everyone looked down at the soaking wet dead man.

"Anyone recognize this guy?" McCormick asked, looking around.

Everyone shook their heads. Then Clifford waved most of the idle cops away to attend to their orders as he squatted down to examine the corpse. McCormick joined him while Simone stood anxiously above and watched.

"What da ya think, Mac?" Clifford asked McCormick.

"Well, judging by what I'm seeing, I'd say somebody stuffed this guy into this gunny sack and was tryin' to sink'em in the river," McCormick replied, pointing to the canvas bag twisted around the legs of the dead man.

"Yeah, looks like it didn't take," Clifford added.

"Nah, they used a rotten bag, see this?" McCormick pointed out, "whatever they used for weight musta split the bottom seam and fell out, causing the body to rise to the surface."

Clifford, nodded in agreement and then carefully began going through the dead man's outer coat pockets, but found nothing useful but wet lint. However, when the surface of the heavy wool coat was examined more carefully they found a ...

"Bullet hole? What da ya think, Mac?" Clifford said pointing it out.

McCormick leaned over for a closer look. "Yep, sure looks like it. Let's get this coat off him."

The coat was unbuttoned and pulled open revealing ...

"Hey, this guy's a cop of some sort," McCormick said in surprise as he gazed at a dark green uniform. The heavy coat was then wrestled off the body revealing two shoulder patches emblazoned with the emblems of the Royal Canadian Border Patrol.

"Well, I'll be dipped. How'd a Canadian border cop get over here?" Clifford commented.

"I'd say prolly in one of them trucks we were supposed to find," McCormick replied, now standing up and wiping off his wet hands on his trench coat. "Wonder what they were shipping."

"I can answer that," Clifford said as he also stood, "Medical supplies."

"Medical supplies?" McCormick replied in surprise.

"Yep, that's what Sal said was in the message he got. Trucks moving medical supplies through here," Clifford answered.

"Quoi? Je ne comprends pas?" Simone rattled off, "I'm sorry. I mean, I don't understand?"

"Medical supplies. You know, what they use in a hospital," McCormick explained.

"Oui, fournitures medicales, I understand now. But why? Why would the Red Hand want medical supplies?" she asked, "and what does Andrea Canard have to do with this?"

"All good questions, detective, wish we had the answers for ya," Clifford said, "but for now, all we got is a dead convicts final message, an empty warehouse, and a dead Canadian cop. This day is turning out to be a real jewel," Clifford grumbled sarcastically.

"So, here's my next question, how many trucks were there, and where are they headin'?" McCormick said.

"Let's check with the warehouse and the port authority management and see who rented this space. They're supposed to keep records," Clifford answered. "Then he motioned for one of the cops to come over. "Officer, I want you to stand post here until the city coroner shows up. Tell him I said I want this guy's prints," he pointed to the dead man, "sent to the Canadian government to find out who he is and, of course, to notify next of kin. I'm sure somebody by now is missin' him."

"Yes, sir, Chief," the officer replied, and then saluted.

"And I want this warehouse gone over and dusted, top to bottom, got it?"

The cop nodded, Clifford grunted in approval and then walked off. "You two comin'?" Clifford barked behind his back. McCormick and Simone hurried to catch up.

Clifford, McCormick and Simone stormed into the Port Authority offices and demanded to see records of who rented the warehouse in question. When the Port Authority manager could not produce what was requested, Clifford had him, along with the entire office staff arrested, handcuffed, and taken out of the building.

"They're either stupid, think I'm stupid, or they're being paid off. Either way, I'm gonna get to the bottom of this," Clifford growled.

"I dunno, Chief," McCormick cautioned, "I don't think City Hall is gonna approve you closing the docks for an empty warehouse and one floater."

Clifford huffed in annoyance. "You're no help, McCormick. What'm I supposed to do?"

"Alright, look, if we're dealin' with who we think we are then there'll be no records of that warehouse ever being used. They're too smart to leave a paper trail. How 'bout we start askin' around and see if any ships left here in the last few days with loaded trucks?"

"You think them trucks are on board a ship?"

"I can't be sure, but why drive all the way here from somewhere in Canada to use a warehouse, and then drive someplace else? This is a port."

"Maybe they transferred the cargo to other trucks?" Clifford suggested.

"Maybe," McCormick reluctantly agreed, "we can check the highways, but my gut is tellin' me they're on the ocean headed somewhere."

"Well, just to make sure I'll have the highway patrol check for a convoy of unregistered trucks … needle in a haystack probably, but it can't hurt. In the meantime, why don't you and Detective Desaraux check out your theory, and then we'll meet back in my office to confer," Clifford suggested, "looks like I'll be callin' the D.A. about this mess. Hope he's in a good mood."

"Better you than me, boss," McCormick added.

"*Oui,* sounds A-OK to me," Simone replied.

McCormick and Clifford winked at each other, and then McCormick took Simone by the elbow and hurried off while Clifford bellowed orders to his men.

Chapter Nineteen

McCormick and Simone spent the remainder of that day interviewing as many remaining Port Authority and Warehouse Authority personal as they could find, and who would voluntarily cooperate, before they would be subject to arrest by the Metropolitan Police Department. Nobody seemed to know, or wanted to know for that matter, anything about unregistered phantom trucks parked in warehouses, or on departing ships. But then there was this one old sailor ...

McCormick had just stepped out of a phone booth in a local dive after calling Maxine to make sure she was alright. She missed him of course, but said the cops were treating her swell and seeing to her needs, and that Fay was stopping by to bring her some supper. McCormick breathed a sigh of relief as he exited the booth, when he noticed Simone speaking with a surly looking man wearing dirty coveralls and a seaman's cap. McCormick walked over to see what was going on.

"Who's your new friend, Simone?" McCormick asked suspiciously.

"Detective Mac, this is *Monsieur* Abbott, who claims to have worked here throughout the war and knows everything there is to know about our *demandes de renseignements*."

"Our what?" McCormick asked.

"*Excuez-moi,* I mean, our in-quiries," she corrected.

"Oh really?" McCormick replied, turning to the short, stocky man, who smelled like a mixture of dirty cloths, sweat, and booze.

"Yeah, that's right," the man, Abbott, croaked in a voice that sounded like sandpaper. "I heard the little lady was askin' questions … not a good idea 'round here," he said looking suspiciously over a shoulder.

"Tell ya what, Mister Abbott, why don't we find us a nice quiet seat and have a chat?" McCormick said, taking Abbott by a bicep and moving him towards a booth at the very back of the place. Simone followed. Once they got there, McCormick nudged Abbott into one side and sat down next to him, while Simone slid into the other.

"I'm talkin' if yer buyin'," Abbott croaked a toothless smile.

"Look, don't waste our time," McCormick said, leaning his shoulder into him, "this lady and I are detectives working a homicide. Now, you volunteered to speak with us, and we appreciate that, but if I feel you're withholding something, I'm gonna haul you downtown and sweat you under some hot lights. Ya got that?" McCormick warned, and jabbing a finger at him.

Abbott swallowed hard and nodded. "Just tryin' to help the little lady out," he nervously replied.

"Please, *Monsieur,* speak with us quickly before more innocent people are killed," Simone urged.

Abbott looked them both over and then began.

"Okay, look, folks, I been working these docks and the ships since I was a runt kid. I know everything there is to know about what goes on 'round here, legal and otherwise, and I've learned over the years to keep my yap shut … until now."

"So, what's changed?" McCormick asked.

"A few months ago some new guys started showin' up. Not from 'round here and not yer average criminal type, if ya knows what I mean … lots of dough behind them, buying off port cops, management, ship captains, some crew … and fer those who don't cooperate with 'em, they disappear. I keep a real low profile and stayed outta their way. Well, what might interest yoos two is what the pretty lady here was askin' about … trucks appearing and disappearin', fleets of 'em, stuffed to the gills with … say I'm really thirsty, how 'bout it?"

McCormick raised his hand and held up a finger. A moment later, a large mug of beer appeared on the table. Abbott's eyes widened at the ice cold brew, but as he reached for the mug, McCormick grabbed his forearm and held it fast.

"You were sayin' these trucks were stuffed with?"

Abbott cursed quietly under his breath. "Red Cross stuff, tons of it, as far as I could tell. Coming in week after week …"

"And heading where?" McCormick pressed.

"Out to sea," Abbott replied.

"Where, *Monsieur,* can you tell us where?" Simone asked, adding her hand from across the table to McCormick's.

"As far as I could figure out, bein' the curious feller that I am, them ships where headin' for Japan or thereabouts."

McCormick released Abbott's arm and Simone took her own hand away as they watched Abbott guzzle down his reward.

"Japan? Wonder why they're shipping that stuff to Japan?" McCormick quietly said to Simone.

"*Je suis confus,* I am as confused as you, *détective.* And the still unanswered question in my mind is: how is Canard involved in all of this intrigue?"

"Ya got me swingin', kid," McCormick replied, scratching the day old stubble on his cheek.

They were then interrupted by the sudden, crude, noisy, and foul smelling burps emanating from Abbott. "Hey, how 'bout round two?" he smiled at his hosts.

"Maybe, later. What else can ya tell us?" McCormick asked.

"Well, sir, I happen to know that at least one of the ships that was carryin' them trucks was a cargo ship I used to be a mate on."

"Okay, and?"

"And, I know what ports that boat stops at, that's what ..." he replied, belching again.

Simone placed a hand over her nose and closed her eyes briefly.

"Okay, so where does this ship make port?" McCormick pressed.

"Last I knew, she put in to the Port of Hakata, took on supplies, or unloaded cargo or crew, and then made Port at Busan," he replied.

"Both in Japan?"

"Nope, jus Hakata. Busan is in South Korea … unless they moved it," he wheezed in laughter.

McCormick grunted in understanding and, again, held up a finger to the delight of Abbott.

"What do you think, Mac?" Simone quietly asked.

"I dunno, yet, but something big is up. It's my experience with these guys that they don't do anything small scale."

"You mean the *La Main Rouge*?"

"No, I'm thinking now that these Red Hand characters are just go-betweens, hired muscle, for the people who are really running the show."

"I do not follow you. Are you saying there are others involved? Who, who are they?"

"I'll tell ya, as soon as we finish with Mr. Abbott here, if we can keep him sober enough that is. Okay, listen, Mr. Abbott, do any of these guys you been seein' hang around here? Would you recognize any of 'em if you saw them?"

Abbott's eyes widened for a moment as he suddenly slouched down into the seat.

"Funny you should ask, shipmate, but two of 'em yer lookin' for just walked in," Abbott said as he pointed with his chin towards the front of the place.

McCormick looked up and saw two men who had just entered from the street. It was obvious from the way they were dressed that they were not locals, and it looked as though they were searching the crowded place for something or someone. Simone began to turn around to look, but McCormick cautioned her not to. The two men began walking towards the back of the room to where the three where sitting. McCormick looked over and told Abbott to get down on the floor, under the table. He quickly did so. Simone mouthed, "How many?" McCormick discreetly held up two fingers. Simone nodded, took a deep breath, stood up, came around the end of the table, and unexpectantly sat down in McCormick's lap. Taking his face in both hands she whispered, "Forgive me," into his ear, and then began passionately kissing him. The two men walked buy without seeming to notice. Simone looked up after they had passed and told McCormick they had gone into *les toilette*. McCormick nodded and lifted Simone off. Then he turned to Abbott and told him to, "Beat it and keep yer head down."

Abbott scurried out of the place like a frightened rat as McCormick turned towards the men's lavatory and quickly told Simone to, "Stay here." And then he marched away.

"Mac, wait," she pleaded, but too late. McCormick pushed the men's room door open and walked inside.

There were several other customers in the dimly lit, smelly bathroom, and it looked as though they were being interrogated by the two strangers who wore dark overcoats, leather gloves, and black fedoras. McCormick acted as casual as he could, as he walked past the men and towards the porcelain urinals that lined one wall. That's when he caught the eye of one of the strangers who seemed to recognize the detective. He quickly said something to his partner in what sounded like French, prompting the other one's hand to disappear into an outer coat pocket. McCormick didn't wait to see what it was the man was reaching for, he just hauled off and plowed him a solid one to the side of his head. The man crumpled to the floor like a rag doll, while his partner, now gun in hand, opened fire at the defenseless detective. Any remaining patrons scattered out the door, dodging hot lead. McCormick took evasive action as he ducked and rolled to avoid being hit. "What'da ya want?" McCormick shouted.

"Toi et la fenne morte," the remaining stranger shouted before he fired, wildly again. McCormick didn't speak French, but he knew just enough Italian to understand the word 'morti' meant 'dead'. Just then another male customer entered, he could have been the bouncer, or the owner of the establishment, either way it didn't matter, the gunman made short work of him with a single shot, giving McCormick just enough time needed to grab up a metal wastepaper can, and hurl it at the assailant, who caught it full in the face.

Seizing the opportunity, McCormick quickly covered the short distance between them and swung with a hard right, his long, powerful arms, knocking the pistol out of the gunman's hand as it discharged one more round into a nearby sink, causing it to explode into pieces. The detective followed that with a savage, left upper-cut, which lifted the gunman off his feet, and sent him sprawling into the tiled wall behind him. "You're under arrest," McCormick shouted as he reached down to further subdue the semi-conscious man. Just then he heard the squeak of the door open behind him. He expected to see another curious customer; however, it was a third gunman, holding out a weapon that was aimed, point blank, at the detective.

"Goodnight cop," were the only words this gunman spoke ... followed by a loud *crack*. McCormick jumped; expecting to feel the impact of a bullet hitting him, but all he saw was the unfired weapon leaving the assailants hand and falling uselessly to the floor. A moment later, the gunman fell onto both knees, his mouth trying to form words, before pitching forward and landing heavily, face first, onto the wet concrete floor. Simone Desaraux stood in the doorway, both arms straight out, and hands gripping a smoking Walther P38.

"Mac, are you A-Okay?

McCormick sighed with relief, and then held up the okay sign with one hand, before turning to the other man who was attempting to get up off the floor.

"Oh no, ya don't," McCormick said as he struck the guy with a hard right cross, sending him back down to the floor in a heap. When McCormick turned around, Simone was standing, seemingly frozen, over the body of the third gunman she had shot; a neat, round hole, oozing red was drilled between his shoulder blades. "Hey, snap out of it," he barked, startling her back to reality, "Keep an eye out in case any more show up."

Simone, now wide-eyed, nodded quickly, turned and watched the door, gun raised to a defensive position while McCormick turned his back to put handcuffs on the unconscious men. A minute or so later, the detectives heard the sound of sirens, as police patrol cars roared up in front of the place.

Chapter Twenty

It was a crowded circus of confused people milling about on the sidewalk, until Chief Clifford arrived via squad car. "Who's in charge here?" he growled at the nearest patrolman as he got out. "Get these civilians away from the entrance, put up some tape, and no reporters inside until I say so."

"Yes sir, Chief," several uniforms replied. Clifford then bullied his way through the front door of the bar as cops inside the place parted the aisle leading to the back of the room. They pointed to McCormick and Simone who were sitting in a booth. Clifford shook his head, gave a few quick orders, and then marched to where the couple sat.

"You two alright?" he asked in concern.

"Oh just dandy, boss," McCormick replied dryly as he rubbed his bruised knuckles.

"*Oui,* we are, as you say, A-O - ..." Simone began to say, when ...

"Detective, if you say, 'A-OK', I'm sending you back to France in a row boat," Clifford retorted, and pointed his tooth-pick at her, "Now, are you injured, detective?"

"No, boss," Simone replied cautiously.

"Well, that's somethin'. I take it some others aren't so lucky?"

Both detectives slowly shook their heads.

Alright, what happened in here?" Clifford asked

"Take'a look for yourself, Chief," McCormick thumb-pointed to the lavatory, where several police officers were standing guard with drawn weapons.

Clifford grunted, shoved the toothpick back into his mouth, and walked into the rest room. After stepping over two bodies, the two unconscious men, handcuffed together, and a badly damaged sink squirting a stream of water up to the ceiling, Clifford cursed under his breath, and then said ...

"Alright, wake those two guys up, get'em off the floor, confiscate any weapons, and stick them both in a squad car," he ordered two of the cops.

The unconscious gunmen were slapped awake and then dragged out of the building, leaving only the bodies of the third gunman and the innocent civilian. After that, McCormick joined Clifford and briefly gave him the nuts and bolts of what happened.

Clifford sighed with relief and squeezed McCormick's shoulder, "Saved your bacon, did she, McCormick?" Clifford quietly said.

"Yeah, Chief, I should be dead right now if it wasn't for her," he replied.

Clifford turned and looked out to where Simone sat at a table with her forehead resting on her hands. "She's had a tough assignment here so far, poor kid, and what just happened complicates things. Anyway, I'm gonna need a detailed report about this mess a.s.a.p., the Assistant Commissioner and the D.A. are gonna wanna know what happened before the papers get a'hold of this. It looks like the O.K. coral in here."

"We're A-OK, Chief," McCormick smirked.

Clifford snorted loudly, "Don't start with me, Mac, it's late and I'm tired ... and you'd better get yourself home to Maxine before she has another fit. She feels left out. I'll take care of things here. I'm gettin' too old for this ya know," Clifford complained.

"I know. Thanks Chief. I'll take Simone home with me and we'll see you in the morning," McCormick said as he walked out.

Chapter Twenty-One

"You'd better start spillin' your guts, mister," Clifford threatened the prisoner, who quietly sat, hand and leg cuffed, in a small interrogation room at police headquarters. Behind the prisoner stood several burly cops holding night-sticks and another armed with a shotgun. "You're already guilty of one murder tonight and if I don't miss my guess, you're one of the guys that broke in here, gassed my officers, and then killed the other prisoners who were members of your gang. Now we're talking about multiple murders. I don't need a jury to tell me that you'll get the chair for this. Is that what you want? Ever see a man die in the chair, huh, have ya? Well it ain't pretty."

The prisoner was a well-built man, in his prime, who merely sat there in his bloodied shirt sleeves and, by all appearances, seemed not to be the least bit intimidated by Clifford's tirade. Though his face was badly bruised and swollen, along with missing several molars due to McCormick's fists, he managed to form a crooked, defiant grin every so often during Clifford's noisy interrogation procedure, which had already lasted most of the night between him and his comrade. Both prisoners' nonchalet demeanors only served to frustrate and anger the Chief to the boiling point. After getting no-where with either men, an exasperated Clifford ordered his officers to throw them into separate cells, and to stand guard over them in shifts. Then he stormed out of the room and headed for the elevator, cursing colorfully.

Meanwhile, McCormick and Simone had arrived hours earlier at the McCormick home where they were greeted by several heavily armed uniforms, along with a police force detective. After baths and a late supper, McCormick made sure Simone was tucked in safely into a spare bedroom, with a cop outside the door, before he and Maxine retired to their bedroom. McCormick yawned heavily, after he turned the night-stand lamp off, and slid into bed next to Maxine. Maxine lay there silently staring at the dim outline of her very swollen tummy.

"Looks like you two had quite a night," she quietly said in the dark.

McCormick cleared his throat, "Well, it could've gone better, that's for sure. But, ya know, I think we're making some headway," he carefully replied to her.

Suddenly, he felt her sharp elbow jab him in the ribs.

"*Ouch*! What'd ya do that for?"

"I saw your knuckles when you came home. You think I dunno know what that means?" Maxine whispered loudly, "And your French detective friend looked like death-warmed-over, all haggard and bleached out. I've seen that look before ... on me, after I had'ta kill a guy. So look, I don't wanna be left in the dark about what's goin' on. We're a team, remember? For better or for worse?"

McCormick sighed, and turned on his side towards her. He placed a large hand gently on top of her belly. The child inside moved happily as if knowing it was daddy saying hello. After removing his hand, he reached for Maxine's face ... it felt wet with tears.

"Hey, cupcake, I'm sorry, okay. I'm just trying not to ..."

"Bring work home?" Maxine laughed and then she snorted. "Like those guys bustin' into our house and us havin' to shoot up our living room?"

"And bathroom," McCormick added.

"Just the door ..."

"And the wall across from the door," McCormick added again.

They both started to laugh as they moved closer together. McCormick put an arm around her as she, with some difficulty, turned on her side to face her husband.

"And here I was thinkin' that we promised we would have nothing come between us," McCormick said, patting her tummy gently.

They both began laughing uncontrollably and trying to shush each other so that the cop outside their door wouldn't overhear. Finally, McCormick cleared his throat and told Maxine the details of the evening's activities at the shipyard bar.

Maxine sighed, "Looks like we owe her big time, huh?"

"Yep, she had my back, thankfully," McCormick replied.

"What happened to those two guys who tried to kill you?" Maxine asked.

"Chief took'em down to headquarters. Let's hope he can sweat somethin' outta them we can use."

After a period of silence went by, McCormick whispered, "Max, you asleep?"

"The Chief won't get anything outta those guys, Mac, you know that," Maxine quietly whispered

"Huh? What'da ya talkin' about? Clifford'll break them cheap hoods like ..."

"Not if they're Dark Circle assassins," she stated grimly.

Now it was McCormick's turn to remain silent for a few minutes, until ...

"Mac, you asleep?" Maxine whispered.

"Not hardly. How did you know?"

"I can feel it ... I can feel *them*. I felt it when you came home tonight. They're back, aren't they, Mac?"

McCormick hesitated, but then spoke freely.

"We think so, that is Sal, me, and the Chief. There's something bigger goin' on than just this French gang that's come to town. We're trying to figure out what their game is, their big plan."

"Yeah, well, just remember, we gave 'em a pretty good black eye last time. They're not gonna forget," Maxine said.

"And that's why I want you as far away from this current mess as we can keep you," McCormick answered, placing a hand on her face.

"I know, sweetheart ... I know ..." and then she began to snore.

McCormick waited until he was sure she was asleep before he turned over onto his back again and stared up into the blackness. He worried what else awaited them in this investigation, how it would affect Maxine ... and his unborn child, and ... And then it was morning.

Chapter Twenty-Two

Later the next day, McCormick, Simone, and Clifford sat in the Chief's office reviewing the events of the previous day ...

"Here's what I don't get," Clifford said, "this guy, Abbott is sayin' that those trucks we're lookin' for are somewhere on a ship headed for Japan? What's that gotta do with all this?"

"Off hand, boss, I dunno, but if it involves the Dark Circle, then it's a major deal. And, according to Abbott, this had been goin' on for a while," McCormick replied, crossing his legs.

"*Pardonnez-moi, Chief,*" Simone interrupted, "but also, let us be concerned with how this beast Canard fits into all of this. I am afraid we are no closer to catching him since my arrival."

"One connects to the other," McCormick said, "Canard belongs to the Red Hand gang, the gang is being used by the Dark Circle, and these guys are plotting something big, as usual."

"Excuez-moi," Simone said, "but who is this *Cercle Noir* you speak of? I have never heard if it."

McCormick and Clifford looked at each other. "Better fill her in, Mac," Clifford said.

And McCormick did. Afterward, Simone just sat in front of the two men in amazement.

"You are not, as you say: 'pulling on my leg', are you?" she asked.

Both men solemnly shook their heads.

"Mon Dieu, what is this world coming to?" she replied, rubbing her forehead.

"It's goin' to hell in a hand basket, that's what, if we don't stay ahead of these guys," Clifford growled.

"Look, detective," McCormick cut in, "I'm now convinced that your Andre Canard is in with, not only, this Red Hand gang, but is being used by the Dark Circle as well. If that's the case, then this is bigger than a man hunt for a murderer. This could very well involve the future of civilization."

"This *Cercle Noir*, Dark Circle, is that powerful?" Simone asked.

"Yeah, it is, based on our experience so far. Now, I'm hopin' that by figuring out what they're up to and throwing a monkey wrench into it, we just might, not only, put this Red Hand gang outta business, but catch this Canard fugitive as well," McCormick said.

"Sounds like a good plan, McCormick, but how do we figure out what they're up to and then stop 'em?" Clifford asked.

"One thing at a time, Chief," McCormick said. "Let's consider what we do know, so far."

"Ok," Clifford began, "we know that the Red Hand is involved somehow in bringing in trucks loaded with medical supplies …"

"From Canada, *oui?*" Simone interjected.

"That's right," McCormick agreed. "That's why that poor border cop was murdered and shipped here."

"We should alert the Canadian authorities' *immédiatement,* perhaps they can stop any more shipments," Simone suggested.

"We could, but that might queer the deal for us on this end. Alert everyone and they'll close up shop, scatter, and then we got zip. No, if we wanna do this right, we gotta catch them in the act, and then follow the bread crumbs to the source," McCormick countered.

"Deal? Zip? Bread crumbs? I do not follow, Mac," Simone replied looking confused.

"He means we gotta be cagey … you know, discreet, sneaky. Don't let 'em know we're comin' until we get all the facts and find their leader," Clifford translated.

"Ah, *oui*, now I understand, *procéder tranquillement*," she replied, holding an index finger against her lips.

"You got it, detective," Clifford congratulated, "now the next thing is how do we go about it?"

McCormick sat back and thought. "Ya know, Chief, Maxine said somethin' to me last night that makes sense today."

"What's that, Mac?"

"So lemme ask ya, have ya got anywhere with our prisoners?"

Clifford snorted with disgust. "Tight as clams and they sure ain't afraid of the law."

"Yeah, just what I thought. Max said if those guys were D.C. agents, they're trained not to blab to the authorities, unless …"

"Unless what, Mac?" Simone asked.

"Unless they're interrogated by people they're *more* afraid of. Remember, Chief?"

It took a moment, but then Clifford raised both eyebrows with recollection. "Hey, you're talkin' about when Maxine was kidnapped?"

McCormick nodded his head.

"Maxine was *kidnappé? Mon dieu*, when?" Simone replied with surprise.

Clifford wrung his face with a hand and then took a long gulp of his coffee. "Later detective. Look, Mac, they've been duly arrested and are in legal custody under heavy guard pending action from the D.A. I just can't hand them over to …"

"Prisoners have been known to escape, haven't they?" McCormick replied as he casually examined his finger nails.

Clifford involuntarily began coughing, then shook his head, stood up, shoved his hands into his pockets, and began to walk around the office. Simone looked curiously at both men.

"Look, boss, if these guys know anything about what's goin' on, then *we* need to know and fast, before more bodies start showin' up," McCormick reasoned.

"So, what'da ya want me to do, just let'em go Scott free?"

"Like I just said, Chief, people escape, and I'm sure we'll get 'em back eventually to stand trial," McCormick said.

"I'm too old for this, McCormick," Clifford lamented as he rubbed his forehead, " …my career … my pension … my wife …"

"My kiester," McCormick added.

Clifford looked over at McCormick, sighed heavily, ran his eyes across the ceiling once or twice, then replied, "Okay, make the call, and God help me."

McCormick stood up and went over to Clifford's desk to use the telephone.

"What is happening, *Monsieur,* Mac, Chief?" Simone asked, sitting on the edge of her chair.

"The end of the world, detective," Clifford answered as he ran a hand through his thinning hair.

"The end of the world?" Simone repeated in confusion.

"Yep, the end of my world if this blows up in my face," Clifford groaned. " ... and I need a drink," he said, going over and opening a bottom drawer of his desk while McCormick spoke to someone on the phone. Clifford unscrewed the cap on the fifth and tipped back a mouthful. He swallowed hard and briefly gasped for breath as he wiped the tears away from his eyes. "Care for a pull, detective?" he asked Simone, offering he the bottle.

"No, Chief, I am on duty," she replied with some indignity.

"Oh great, a choir girl," he remarked as he took another pull.

"All set, Chief," McCormick said as he hung the phone up, "all we gotta do is make sure the henhouse is unguarded."

Clifford rolled his eyes again and was about to polish off the rest of the bottle when McCormick went over and took it away from him.

"Blast it, McCormick," Clifford growled.

"You ain't fired yet and you gotta bad heart, remember?" McCormick sternly reminded him. "So, let's all just keep our shirts on and see this through."

Simone now stood up and angrily stomped a foot. "*Detective, Mac, un Chief,* I have never, how did you say, *enlever ma chemise,* taken off my shirt to further an *enquête* … oh, what is word? Ah! Investigation. Nor will I in the future …" she rattled on.

McCormick and Clifford looked at each other and began to laugh. Simone put both hands on her hips and began to tap her foot.

"Oh, boy, that looks familiar," Clifford guffawed, as he now began to weave.

"Sit down, will ya, Chief," McCormick replied as he reached over and pushed the red button on the desk intercom. "Fay, coffee, pronto," he barked.

"Coming right up, uhh, Chief … McCormick, is that you?" Fay responded.

"Yeah, Fay, just bring the coffee. Thanks." McCormick let go of the button, then pointed at Clifford, and then to the empty chair in front of the desk. Clifford got the message, snorted rudely, and sat down heavily into the seat. Fay walked in a second or so later with a steaming mug of coffee. McCormick pointed at Clifford.

"Oh, gimmy that," Clifford growled, taking the mug and shoving his top lip into it.

"Why do I smell liquor?" Fay asked, putting her hands on her hips and looking down at Clifford.

"Don't star with me," Clifford said coming up for air, "and bring me another."

Fay shook her head and left the office.

"Look Simone," McCormick began as he gestured for her to sit back down, "we're about to do something that's a little illegal. So, the Chief and I are giving you the opportunity to just walk outta here, no hard feelings, and let us handle this. If and when we find Canard, we'll turn him over to you."

Simone stood there, shaking her head, back and forth, "No, no, no, that will not do *monsieur,* I will not abandon this chase, *comprend moi?* Whatever has to be done, has to be done. I have come too far and have already spilled blood because of this beast. Now, tell me, what is it you are planning?"

McCormick encouraged her, again, to sit back down, and then he filled her in. When he was finished, Simone put a hand to her mouth and swallowed hard. *"Mon Dieu,* what you are suggesting, it will be *prison pour nous,* prison for us all if we are caught, and the certain end to our careers," she said soberly.

"You got that right," Clifford replied, burped, and then took another gulp of coffee.

Fay entered again with a fresh cup of java, switched cups with Clifford, winked at McCormick, and then quickly left.

Simone took a deep breath and smiled as best she could. *"Non quoi?* Now what? What is our next move?"

McCormick put his hands into his trouser pockets and walked around from behind the desk. "Well, you and I are gonna make ourselves scarce for the time being. We'll keep busy tracking down a few loose ends, and I need to stop in on Max. Chief, you know what you need to do, right?" McCormick said, now standing in front of Clifford.

Clifford looked up, red-eyed. "Yeah, Mac, I'll get it done. And I don't wanna know where this is gonna take place, ya hear? I'm gonna have all I can do to deal with the mess this is gonna cause around here," Clifford grumbled colorfully.

"Yeah, I know, ignorance is bliss, Chief. You let Simone and me handle the rest, ok?" McCormick replied.

"*Oui, Chief,* A-O-K," Simone added, but then she caught herself.

Clifford unexpectantly began to chuckle at her as he slowly shook his head, but then held up the ok gesture to her.

"C'mon, detective, let's get outta here," McCormick said as he headed for the office door. "We'll be in touch Chief," he said to Clifford's back as he held open the door for Simone to walk through.

"Will he be alright?" Simone whispered as she walked by. They both stopped to look back at Clifford who just sat there, unmoving. He just stared into his empty coffee cup ... but then, suddenly ...

"Fay! Coffee. Pronto." he bellowed.

McCormick nodded at Simone, took her by the elbow, and closed the door behind them.

Chapter Twenty-Three

It was a little after three in the morning when Chief Clifford's bedroom telephone rang.

"Oh, Dewy, who could that be at his hour," Mable Clifford snorted and turned over. Clifford sat on the edge of the bed, reached over, and picked up the receiver.

"Clifford ... What? When? I'll be right there," he answered and then hung up.

"What's wrong, dear?" Mable asked as she sat up.

"There's trouble down at the precinct jail. I gotta go," he replied, and then he got up, dressed, and left the house. When Clifford arrived, he was escorted by some uniforms to where the prisoners are kept ... or were kept.

"Alright, report," Clifford blustered.

"They're all gone, Chief, every last one," an officer answered.

"What'da ya mean, gone?"

"Escaped, Chief, all the prisoners ... the drunks, the hookers, the addicts, those two men involved in that bar shooting ... gone."

"How'd they break out?" Clifford barked.

"We don't know, Chief. Clancy was on night duty and everything was locked down. When O'Doul came in to relieve him, he found Clancy tied and gagged behind his desk and all the cells empty," the officer reported.

"Are you tellin' me nobody on duty saw them leave? There's only one way down here, fer Pete's sake," Clifford replied angrily.

"Well, not really, boss. Come with me," the officer said as he walked to the very rear of the cell block, through a long, narrow hallway, and into a storage room. Clifford followed knowing full well what they were going to find. They were met by several other cops and detectives who were crowded around quite a large, square, opening in the stone wall that fresh air was blowing through.

"What's this?" Clifford feigned surprise.

"A secret doorway leading to the alley in back where some of the squad cars are parked. Who would'a figured this was here all these years?"

"Well, this is just great," Clifford cursed, "another black eye for the department. The D.A. and the Commissioner are gonna have my scalp, and I'm gonna have yours if those prisoners aren't caught, pronto."

"We got every available man out lookin', Chief," a sergeant replied nervously.

"You'd better have. I'll be in my office and I want hourly reports. And get somebody down here a.s.a.p. to permanently plug up that hole," Clifford ordered.

"Yes, sir, Chief," the cops saluted. Clifford returned the salute, turned away, and headed for his office, grumbling to himself: "You'd better know what yer doin', McCormick."

Chapter Twenty-Four

It was a dimly lit parlor in an old farmhouse somewhere out in the rurals. In the center of the barely furnished room sat two hooded men, back to back, in metal chairs that were nailed to the wood floor. The two men were both held fast by leather straps, synched tightly across their bare chests. Their ankles also were fastened in a similar way to prevent movement, and their hands were handcuffed behind them. They both puffed and struggled against their bonds to get free as they gasped for air under the dirty and smelly canvas hoods that covered their heads. The men spoke and cursed to each other in fluid French as they tried to make sense out of their current predicament. They wondered why and who had broken them out of the police jail. At first they entertained the idea that they were being rescued by their comrades, but when each received a crippling punch in the stomach, hoods pulled over their heads, followed by being unceremoniously shoved into the trunk of a car, and then transported to wherever they were, they quickly understood otherwise.

After a few more minutes of fruitless struggling, they heard the sound of a door being unlocked and opened. Then they heard multiple, heavy footsteps, enter the room and move towards them. Whoever they were they whispered to one another, not it English or French, but in what sounded like Italian. Suddenly, the hoods were yanked off their heads. Immediately their eyes were assaulted by a blinding white light coming from two flood lamps on each side of them.

"Qu'est-ce que tu veux?," one of the prisoners panted.

"Wadda we want, Frenchy?" replied a heavy voice, just beyond the lights, "we want answers, and you're gonna give them to us, or else, *capire?* Now, why don't we all speak English. You boys know how'ta do that, don't yas?" the voice asked.

"Vous n'obtiendrez aucune coopération de notre part!" The other prisoner spat vehemently.

"I see," the voice replied, "Vinnie, Louie, I don't think I'm getting' through to these mooks. Tell ya what, I'm gonna step out and use the can, when I come back I'd like a little respect, okay?"

One set of footsteps were heard leaving the room and shutting a door. Then the two men heard the squeaking sounds of tight leather gloves being put on.

"Which one ya want, Louie?" one of the remaining two men asked the other.

"Uh, guess, I'll take this guy," Louie replied, standing in front of the nearest prisoner to him.

"Ok then, I'll take this jerk," Vinnie responded with a chuckle. "Hey, do you two guys like roller coasters?" he asked the prisoners. The two confused Frenchmen twisted their necks to try to look at each other.

Then Louie answered, "'Cuz yoos in for quite a ride."

With that statement, there was no more conversation, just the harsh sounds of heavy, neck wrenching, slaps. After about fifteen minutes or so, Sal Canale walked back into the room and he wasn't alone. Vinnie and Louie stopped what they were doing and stood aside. The two prisoners, now drenched with sweat and half conscious, sat there with their chins resting on their chests.

"Better give 'em some water, Sal said. Vinnie and Louie went and got some from a pitcher somewhere in the room and, after grabbing a handful of hair, poured it down the Frenchmen's' throats. Any remaining water was splashed into their faces to revive them. They both coughed and sputtered as they looked around. "Lose the lights," Sal ordered. The flood lamps were extinguished and moved to the side, leaving the room dimly lit by a single table lamp in the corner. The two prisoners now saw a short, stocky, somewhat rotund, older man wearing a nice suit standing there looking down at them. Next to him stood two other younger, taller men, dressed in shirt sleeves, wearing shoulder holsters, and tight fitting leather gloves. There were also two others present, a large, well-built man, and a pretty brunet, who they both recognized from ...

"*Vous!*" they both exclaimed at the same time.

"English," the older man ordered, "or I'll have my boys work yas over some more."

Vinnie and Louie both snickered and slapped their fists into the palms of their other hand.

"No, no ... no more," one prisoner replied.

"Well that's good," Sal said, "now, I understand that you idiots tried to kill these two fine people," Sal gestured to McCormick and Simone, "who, by the way, are my friends. I don't like that. So, here's what you're gonna do. You mooks are gonna answer, truthfully, all their questions. If you don't, or if I even think you're lyin', I'm gonna hurt you where it don't grow back, *capire?*"

Both men, breathing heavily, reluctantly nodded.

"Good. Now, McCormick, ask your questions," Sal said stepping back.

McCormick stepped closer to the nearest one to him and leaned in. "Who do you work for?" he asked.

The Frenchman spat to one side, set his swollen jaw, and looked defiantly up at McCormick. McCormick stepped around to the other prisoner and asked the same question, and got basically the same response.

"Tell yas what," Sal said addressing McCormick, "why don't yoos two take-a walk. There's food in the kitchen."

McCormick nodded, took Simone by the arm and led her out of the room, closing the door behind them.

"Mac, I am sorry, but this method is highly irregular," Simone objected, now hearing the sounds of a beating coming from behind the door.

"C'mon, detective, let's go see if we can scare up a sandwich," McCormick answered as he began to move away.

"This does not bother you? What those men are doing in there?" she said, and pointing with her head behind her.

McCormick stopped abruptly, turned, and placed two beefy hands on her shoulders.

"Look, you have no idea what these people are like, and what they're capable of. Human life means nothing to them, just like this Canard fella you're after. So lemme ask ya, if Andre Canard was sitting in one of those chairs in there, would you be as sympathetic to the man who murdered your father and how many others?"

"No, *monsieur,* I would not. However, that is not my *prérogative.* I am an officer of the law, and bound by duty and tradition to bring men such as Andre Canard to justice. I am neither judge, nor executioner, *comprendre?*"

McCormick huffed with annoyance and squeezed her shoulders. "Nobel words young lady. But are ya gonna stand there and try to convince me you wouldn't've shot Canard down like a dog back in that Paris alley if you had the chance?"

"That would have been self-defense, as it was back at your house, and in that *salle de bar.* However, given the choice, I would be obligated to arrest them, as I said."

"The law and the courts have limitations in this life, detective. These people we're fighting are powerful and well organized. They own politicians, judges, cops. They're insulated from the legal process of the law. Ya know, I was like you not that long ago, but when someone I loved was taken by force from me, I decided my oaths to the law no longer cut it. So, I decided then, as I do now, to use whatever means to fight fire with more fire, for the greater good. It ain't pretty, but lemme tell ya, sister, it works. Now, like we asked you back in the Chief's office, if you gotta problem with all this I'll take you back to my place, or to your hotel, or to the airport, for that matter, if that's what you want, and you can do it your way ... see how far you get. But don't stand there and be a self-righteous cop. You'll just get in the way. I'm gonna take these guys down, with or without your assistance, or approval, got it?"

McCormick gave her shoulder's a final squeeze, and then he walked away, leaving the French detective standing alone in the dark hallway, visibly shaken, and consumed with conflicting emotions. After a few dark minutes in contemplative thought, she was interrupted by a very large man who approached her carrying what appeared to be a large battery along with a set of jumper cables draped around his neck. Simone stepped aside as the gorilla passed her.

" 'Cuse me lady," he grunted, as he walked by and then entered the room where the two prisoners were.

"Mon Dieu," she said under her breath as she hurried to find McCormick. The detective was busy stuffing his face with a ham on rye he had made from the ingredients he found in a refrigerator in the small kitchen. Simone approached and cleared her throat. McCormick turned his head and asked. "Are ya hungry? Help yourself," he said.

Simone did so, making herself a similar sandwich. After a few more minutes of eating and shared silence, Simone spoke. "I apologize for my, how did you say: 'self-righteous' position on this current matter. It is just the way we French are and how my papa taught me, *comprendre?* I do not wish you to be offended if we are to continue to work together."

"Do you?" McCormick asked, "Do you want to continue to work together? Don't you think the Chief and I understand the risk we're taking doing what we're doing? But the way we see it, it's the only way, or people die … a lot of people."

Simone rubbed her forehead with one hand as if she had a headache. Then she sighed and replied. *"Oui, détective,* I am with you despite my *appréhension* and my, I suppose, *naïve* sense of morality. Let us then do what we must to end this."

McCormick nodded and offered her a glass of milk. Simone smiled and accepted it.

"So, Mac, are we, A-OK?" she grinned.

McCormick chuckled at her. "Yeah, sure, A-OK."

Just then, Vinnie stepped into the room. "I think we might'a had'a break through. Sal wants yas to come back."

Chapter Twenty-Five

McCormick and Simone put down their beverages and followed Vinnie back through the hall to the parlor where the two prisoners sat with heads slumped forward in exhaustion, while Louie and the gorilla that had passed Simone in the hallway earlier, gathered up the jumper cables, along with the now spent truck battery.

"Welcome back," Sal said, looking pleased with himself as the two entered the room. "I think maybe now you should try askin' your questions again."

"Alright," McCormick replied. Then he stepped over to the nearest prisoner. "One more time, who're you workin' for?"

The prisoner groaned unpleasantly as he slowly raised his head off his chest. After licking his lips, he spoke: "We are agents of an organization called the Dark Circle ... water, please ...

Sal nodded at Louie who gave the man a drink. Afterward, McCormick continued. "What're you doin' in our town?"

The other prisoner now angrily spoke up, warning his partner of the apparent consequences of what he was doing. With that, Louie stepped forward and drove a fist into his bare stomach.

"Shad-dap," Louie ordered, "you speak when you're asked." Louie then stepped back, and nodded for McCormick to continue. Simone just stood behind everyone, eyes closed, one arm across her belly, while the other hand was pinching the bridge of her nose.

"Again, what is the Dark Circle doing in this town?" McCormick repeated.

The prisoner shook his head in disbelief at what he was about to divulge, but replied: "We are transporting cargo from Canada, *Québec*, to this coast to be shipped overseas."

"Where?"

"South Korea, through Japan," he muttered.

"Medical supplies right?"

The man nodded.

"That's verifies what that Abbott character was tellin' us," McCormick said, looking back at Simone who nodded in agreement.

"Why?" McCormick continued.

"We are not privy to that information. We are just solders following orders."

"Like them Nazi, mooks, right?" Sal cut in.

McCormick held up a hand in caution to Sal, then resumed.

"Tell us what you do know. You must've heard somethin'? So spill it, or my lady friend and I leave the room again," McCormick threatened.

"No, no, stay," the prisoner pleaded.

Just then Vinnie reentered the room. "Whud I miss?" he asked cheerfully.

The other prisoner now got his voice back and, again warned his partner, very graphically, of the fate that awaited him if he didn't ...

"Vinnie, shut this idiot up," Sal ordered.

Vinnie came around and stood in front of the cursing Frenchman, pulled back, and then drove his gloved fist, hard, across his already swollen jaw, knocking him out cold. Vinnie stood back, smiled to himself in approval, and then went over to stand next to Louie who nodded at him with appreciation.

"Please, continue, detective," Sal urged.

"Well?" McCormick said to the prisoner.

The prisoner panted angrily, more at himself than at his tormentors, but he answered.

"I don't know how true this is, but I overheard one of our superiors speak of a war starting over there in the next few months ... and something about making millions providing medical supplies."

"A war? There's no war in South-East Asia," McCormick answered, looking over at Sal who simply shrugged his shoulders.

"Not yet," the prisoner replied, but soon.

McCormick ran the back of his hand across his mouth and resumed.

"Lemme get this straight, the Dark Circle is tryin' to start a war so they can do what? Cash in on selling medical supplies? So this is a money makin' scam? I don't buy it."

"I don't know ... I do not know, *Monsieur,* " the prisoner pleaded, his body now shaking from trauma, "all I know is it's going to happen, and soon."

"These medical supplies, how'd you get'em? Were they stolen?"

"No, we own manufacturing facilities in Canada, this country, and in Europe," he replied.

"Et la, France?" Simone suddenly asked.

Óui, France too," he answered.

"How does *le gang de la Main Rouge,* the Red Hand gang fit into this?" Simone continued. McCormick stood back as Simone came forward. "Answer me."

The prisoner coughed up a little blood from a split lip, but answered.

"They were hired as a *liaison* to expedite matters between transactions in Europe and North America since they have already established a network in both regions."

"I thought the Dark Circle already had Europe and America sewed up?" McCormick interjected.

The prisoner chuckled briefly. Not everything is as it seems. Too many irons in many fires, as you Americans' are fond of saying."

"What does that mean?" McCormick pressed.

"It means we have our enemies to deal with," the prisoner replied with disgust.

"You mean like Victoria Mayhill?" McCormick asked.

The prisoner looked as though he had just been slapped again. He looked up at McCormick with fire in his eyes. "Look, cop, I am already a dead man. However, if you want my continued cooperation, *monsieur,* you will not speak of that woman to me, or of her people."

"Alright then, let's talk about this Red Hand gang," McCormick continued, "how they are helping you in this town?"

"They are facilitating transportation and shipping overseas," he replied.

"Wait-a minute," Sal now interrupted, "we, that is, the Families control the trucking throughout this state. Ain't no way we're helpin' any outside mob to transport their stuff without our okay."

"You are mistaken, *monsieur,* the Red Hand has already made a deal with one of your so called 'Families' in this matter. Perhaps you should pay more attention to your own business than to ours, eh?"

Sal, came forward ready to strike the prisoner with the back of his hand when McCormick prevented him.

"Easy, Sal, plenty of time for that," McCormick said.

"Just say the word, Sal, and we'll put some holes in these guy's heads," Vinnie said as he and Louie reached for their guns.

Sal held up a hand. "Nah, let's find out who the rat is first," Sal replied, looking at the prisoner, "So, who we talkin' about? Gotta name? Spill it, or else," he threatened.

The Frenchman closed his eyes and thought for a moment, and then he replied, "We've dealt with a mobster named, Igino … and some others."

"Igino?" Sal said in surprise.

"Hey, ain't that big Tony Barbasonti's right hand guy?" Louie piped in.

"Yeah, it sure sounds like it," Sal replied with subdued astonishment, "We'll see about this later. Please continue detective."

McCormick turned back to Simone. "Anything more you wanna ask?"

Simone looked at the prisoner. "Does the name, Andre Canard mean anything to you?" she asked.

The Frenchman's eyes widened. "Yes ... and I regret that he is French. He is an animal, but he has resources to exploit."

"Have you seen him? Do you know where he is?"

"I don't know his location. He is a ghost," the prisoner responded.

"I want him, do you understand? *Dis moi quelque chose,* tell me something," she exploded into his face. "Tell me! *Dîtes-moi, Dîtes-moi!*"

"I don't know, I tell you ... but my partner may. He has had dealing with him *personnellement.*"

"Take it easy, detective," McCormick said, pulling her away.

"I wish to speak with this other man. Wake him, *à present,*" she demanded looking over at Sal.

Sal grinned and turned to Vinnie and Louie, "You heard the lady, wake this mook up."

The two hoods went over, grabbed a handful of the other Frenchman's hair, and began to slap him awake. Louie brought over water and splashed it into his face. After a few moments, and a few more slaps, the other prisoner woke up with difficulty, working his almost dislocated jaw back and forth a few times before spitting a glob of blood onto the wood floor.

"Rise and shine sweetheart," Louie wisecracked, "time to answer some questions, or we're gonna hook you up to that battery again, got it?" he said, giving the man's face a shove.

Vinnie let go of his hair, and then they both stood back and waited. Sal nodded to Simone. She walked over and stood in front of the second prisoner.

"You will answer my questions, *monsieur,* or there will be severe consequences, *comprenez vous*?"

This Frenchman, who was apparently tougher than his counterpart, both in looks and in temperament, stared up at Simone with utter contempt. *"Police Française, oui?* he asked.

"Oui, la Sûreté," Simone responded. "Now, speak in English and answer my questions."

"You *pouffiasse,* I will take great pleasure in making you curse your mother for giving you birth … you filthy …"

Simone lunged at him, striking his unprotected face with her bare fists with all she could muster and screaming insults.

"Simone!" McCormick shouted, coming over and pulling her off the prisoner. "Calm down, detective, this is getting us nowhere. Calm down," he said, and shaking her.

Simone angrily shrugged off McCormick's grip and then quietly stepped to the other side of the room to regain her composer and fix her disheveled hair. The prisoner just laughed with sadistic amusement as he spit blood from a variety of fingernail scratches and a broken nose. Suddenly, Vinnie pulled the weapon from his shoulder holster, went over and placed the end of the barrel against the forehead of the bleeding Frenchman. He cocked the hammer back, and then looked at Sal for permission.

"Do not kill him yet," Simone shouted for the other side of the room, "I am not finished questioning him."

Sal shrugged. Vinnie understood and removed the weapon from the man's head. "Lucky," Vinnie said, leaning into the Frenchman's face. Then he punched him a good one in the guts. "Be nice to the lady, ya hear?" he whispered, and then he returned to stand next to his partner.

The Frenchman was coughing up a lung as Simone returned and, again, stood before him.

"This is what I purpose," she said, calmly, "you will answer my questions with regard to the murderer, Andre Canard. If you do so, you will be sent to prison. If you do not, you will be set free."

Sal and McCormick looked at each other with concern, but said nothing.

The Frenchman, began to laugh again, despite his injuries, "You say you will free me, *madam,* if I do not answer your questions?" he asked in disbelief.

"*Oui,* you will be set free and we will send out word ahead of you that you have cooperated fully with us in our investigation. Now, *monsieur,* how long do you think you will last when your criminal organization finds this out, eh? Apparently, the torture my friends have performed on you does not work, and as far as I am concerned, a bullet is too good for you. And so, let us see what your people will do to you? You have one minute to decide ... begin," she said, looking at her wrist watch and tapping a foot.

"You are bluffing," the Frenchman accused as he looked around the room ... but everyone just stared back at him.

"Don't be a fool. You've seen what they do to traitors," the other prisoner said.

"Tais toi! Shut up! *You* are the traitor."

"Thirty seconds," Simone announced.

"May be so, but at least I will be alive in a prison if I cooperate. What is the alternative, eh? Surgically turned inside out and hung by our ..."

"Shut up! Shut up!" the other man yelled.

"Time is up," Simone announced, "cut him loose and deposit him in the city. Let him walk to his companions."

Sal nodded to his guys and Louie took out a pocket knife.

"No! Wait, wait, let me speak," the Frenchman now begged.

"Speak then. Tell me where Andre Canard can be found, *vite*," Simone shouted down at him.

"He … he and his mutt bodyguard are hiding in a rented house on the west side of this city, near the power plant, but he does not stay in one location long, he moves around …"

"Give us specific directions, now," Simone pressed as she took out a small notebook and a pencil. The prisoner rattled off several locations and then hung his head and cursed. Then McCormick joined Simone.

"How do ya know so many specifics about this guy?" he inquired.

"Our superiors do not trust him. And so they had us watch him. They fear he is unstable and draws too much attention. As soon as our business is concluded with him, and the Red Hand, we have been told someone would be sent to eliminate him."

McCormick and Simone looked at each other.

"No. Not until I have arrested or killed him myself," Simone replied firmly. "Now, how long before your business is concluded with Canard and his gang?"

"There is one more large shipment due to come in within the next few days," the other prisoner volunteered, "after that, this pipeline will be abandoned, and all remaining assets turned over to the Red Hand as part of payment for their help."

"And how do your people plan on pullin' that off when the mob here is in control of these things?" Sal interjected.

The other Frenchman answered. "The mobs in this town are over, or soon will be. The Red Hand will control everything, and you relics will be forced to cooperate, or else. You have no idea of who you are dealing with now. The Circle has given them resources that will assure that the mobs will cooperate ... or simply cease to exist."

"Oh, yeah, well I got news for yas, that ain't gonna happen, ya see? That Zhenobia broad tried it a few years back and now she's worm food," Sal blustered.

"Ah yes, Madam Zhenobia," the prisoner, replied, "we have learned much from her mistakes. We won't make the same ones again. I suggest you find another line of work," he laughed.

Now Louie, pulled his gun, "Hey, Sal, lemme plug 'em, will ya?" he said.

Sal held up a hand. "Knock it off. I promised Chief Clifford we'd take good care of these guys for him and that's exactly what we're gonna do just as soon as we squeeze every last bit of information outta them, *capire*?"

Chapter Twenty-Six

All things considered, it wasn't a bad plan. A four pronged, sneak attack, coordinated clandestinely through Chief Clifford, who had received an anonymous tip that a convoy of illegally registered trucks was heading their way smuggling contraband and were being loaded on to a particular ship bound for the Orient. Clifford had arranged for armed police officers at the docks to arrest the drivers and confiscate the trucks. He also had the Coast Guard on standby in case the target ship weighed anchor and tried to escape out of the harbor.

Meanwhile, McCormick, Simone and about a dozen heavily armed uniforms and detectives, staked out the locations given to the police department where the fugitive Andre Canard might be holding up, through yet, another anonymous tip.

Finally, Sal Canale, along with Nicky Beonverdella, quietly contacted the Dons' of the other families and explained the situation concerning the Red Hand gang. He also called to their attention the disloyal 'rat' in their mist who was selling out the trucking industry to these foreigners.

A few days later, it all seemed to go down at once.

The fog couldn't be any thicker at the harbor when the first semi-truck pulled up to a particular warehouse entrance. It was followed by six more that formed a line behind it. The driver of the first truck sounded his air horn briefly, and then waited. After a moment, the massive warehouse door began to ascend, prompting the drivers to slowly move their rigs into the interior and park next to each other. Once that had been accomplished, all the drivers got out and stood in front of their trucks, headlamps lighting the area in front of them. The seven drivers stood there silently as the fog continued to roll in through the maw of the still open warehouse entrance.

After a minute or so, one driver whispered to another, "Hey, why ain't they closein' the door?"

"I dunno. I just wanna get paid and get outta here," returned the reply.

"Hey, what's that?" another driver said, pointing in front of him.

What the drivers saw was a line of human figures coming through the dense fog. As the figures got closer, the drivers all recognized that the men coming towards them were ...

"Cops!" several shouted at once.

One driver pulled a gun and was about to shoot when he was cut down, instantly, by machinegun fire.

"This is the Police. Nobody move!" blared a commanding voice from a bullhorn. The drivers all held their hands high over their heads as the officers stormed forward, handcuffs in hand. Chief Clifford, holding the bullhorn, watched in satisfaction as his men subdued and arrested the drivers. As the prisoners were hauled away, Clifford ordered the trailers opened. Bolt cutters appeared, padlocks were severed, and the double doors of each trailer was flung open revealing crates and boxes emblazoned with a Red Cross stacked floor to ceiling.

"Well, they ain't gettin' this load," Clifford said with satisfaction to the officers standing nearby. "Alright, I want this place secured and this contraband inventoried. Now, let's see who's on that ship."

Across town, McCormick, Simone, and two other plain clothed officers, sat in a sedan with headlights off. They had just pulled up outside a house located on dimly lit side street across from a public park.

"Well, this is the place," McCormick said, looking out the front window.

"Only one of the places he could be," Simone corrected, "perhaps the other officers will capture him at their locations.

"Yeah, well, maybe we'll get lucky," McCormick replied optimistically. "Everybody ready?" he asked. The small group checked their weapons and then nodded. "Okay, let's get this guy."

The four, as quietly as they could, left the car and were greeted by four other heavily armed police officers hurrying up the sidewalk towards them.

"Okay, you guys secure the back of the place and be careful," McCormick said to the men. They all nodded and disappeared across the small front lawn.

"Let's go," McCormick whispered to his group, and they all headed for the front entrance. When they got there, they spread out on each side, while McCormick, weapon at the ready, put his ear against the door. On hearing nothing, he shook his head towards the others, and then tried the knob … it wasn't locked. McCormick held his breath and pushed … the door opened easily. Pushing it wide open, the four quickly entered, arms out stretched and pistols cocked. The place was dark and smelled like tobacco smoke. McCormick felt a hand on his arm.

"That is French cigarette odor," Simone whispered. McCormick nodded and moved forward. Every room was checked on the downstairs floor, but they found nothing. Now they gave their attention to a set of stairs leading to a second floor. McCormick pointed at it, and the group moved towards them. Then they began the assent, trying to be as quiet as conditions would allow. When the four had almost reached the second floor landing, one of the last steps squeaked at little too loudly, causing McCormick to hold up a hand and listen, but he heard nothing. When they had reached the landing they found themselves in a hallway with several doors on each side of it, most likely bedrooms. They all moved cautiously forward a few feet, but then squatted in the semi-darkness waiting for McCormick to make a decision on which room to investigate first. Then suddenly, they heard something metallic hit the floor and bounce towards them from farther down the hall. A moment later, they were assaulted by an ear piercing pop, followed by a flash of brilliant white light which instantly blinded everyone.

"Get back!" McCormick yelled. That's when he felt something hard hit his head, knocking him flat onto the hallway runner. At that same moment, he heard Simone scream just before he blacked out.

Simone, blinded and staggering, waved her weapon wildly in front of her in an attempt to find a target. However, that proved impossible since the hallway was now flooded by shimmering white light. Then the gun was knocked out of her hand and she felt herself lifted into the air and draped over someone's shoulder. At first, she thought it was McCormick carrying her to safety, but she soon recognized the pungent smell of French tobacco. Semi-realizing what was happening, she began to thrash and scream as only a frightened woman can, but another person, obviously following from behind, grabbed her by her hair and hit her jaw with something hard, causing her to black out. When she regained consciousness, she found herself outside in the cool night air, lying on her stomach on soft grass. She had a headache, and the side of her swollen face hurt. She managed to get up onto her knees to look around. Though her head was still swimming, and her eyesight had not fully returned, she realized that she had been deposited into a park surrounded by trees. She groaned as she sat down heavily and placed a hand on her forehead trying to remember what happened that caused her to end up here. Then she remembered, "McCormick," she blurted out loud. That's when someone from behind skillfully wrapped a cord of some kind around her neck, and lifted her right off the ground. The assailant was powerful. Pressing her body into his and pulling the cord tighter. Simone gasped for breath as she struggled in her attackers grip. The only thing she realized that was saving her was her left hand that was caught between the cord and her neck.

"Tu me cherches, mademoiselle?" A man's voice, reeking of tobacco, whispered into her right ear.

Simone stiffened as she realized, to her horror, that she was now in the murderous grip of, Andre Canard.

"*Oui,* you filthy pig, I have found you at last," Simone croaked as best she could as she stood on her tip-toes trying her best to breath.

"I believe you have that backward, my dear Detective Desaraux. It is I that have found you, and now you are mine to do with as I wish," Canard replied, pulling harder on the cord in his leather gloved hands. "Perhaps I shall deprive you of both of your beautiful ears before I end your life, hmm, what do you think, *chérie?*"

Simone began to thrash and kick, but to no avail as the cord around her neck became tighter and she realized her hand was now bleeding, feeling the warmth of her blood tricking down her left arm towards her elbow.

"Tell your papa, *allô* for me when you see him," Canard said as he laughed cruelly next to her face. Suddenly, another man's voice interrupted Canard.

"*Monsieur,* we must leave, now. The police are in the park, they are coming," the other voice said with great urgency.

Canard cursed vehemently into Simone's ear, but finally said, "Until next time, *au revoir* …"

The cord was quickly unwound from around Simone's neck and badly bleeding hand, and then she was roughly shoved to the ground, gasping for every breath. A moment later she heard the sounds of running footsteps and another familiar man's voice shouting, "Simone? Simone?" It was McCormick.

"*Ici, ici* … here, I am here," she called out as best she could. Then she felt other hands lift her up into strong arms.

"Simone, are you alright? Somebody call an ambulance, she bleeding," McCormick shouted.

"Is she wounded?" another man's voice asked.

"Dunno, just get that wagon here and search the park. Move!" McCormick ordered, as he cradled her in his arms. Simone's eyes fluttered and she felt herself falling into a deep, dark hole. The last thing she heard before the blackness engulfed her was ...

"Hang in there, detective, I got ya."

Chapter Twenty-Seven

Sal Canale and Nicky Beonverdella sat in two wooden chairs in a well-kept wine cellar. The spacious cellar had plenty of lighting, so that the rows of imported and domestic bottles of wines, some quite rare, could be easily identified and removed from the shelves that lined most of the walls. There were also casks of varying sizes stored in the back of the room near the stairs that ascended up to the restaurant that was unexpectantly closed for the evening due to a water leak, or so the customers were told. Sal and Nicky small talked, while two others behind them, Vinnie and Louie, each stood cradling a submachine gun. After a while, a half-dozen or so mature men came down the stairs and approached Sal and Nicky. When they got near enough, they stopped and eyeballed Vinnie and Louie.

"Hey, Sal, an older one in the group said, "you expectin' trouble?"

Sal chuckled as he sipped on his glass of imported wine, "Nah Tommy, it's just a precaution. We got company comin'," Sal replied.

"Yeah, we wuz told. So, what's the big deal yoo was talkin' about, huh? This is my poker night."

Some of the others nodded and grumbled. Sal motioned with a free hand for them all to 'take it easy,' "I think you'll find our little get together tonight entertaining, trust me," Sal reassured them.

"Yeah," Nicky added, "tonight's gonna be full of surprises. Pull up some furniture and take'a load off." he suggested.

The men, the Dons, the heads of their respective families, looked irritated, but acquiesced as they found empty chairs and sat down.

"So, you think we're being sold out by some of our own?" one of the other Dons asked.

"Yeah," Sal replied.

"And I suppose you got proof?" another asked.

"Yeah, Carlo ... relax," Sal said.

"And when we gonna see this proof?"

"Real soon ... Have some wine," Sal offered, and pointed to an open bottle surrounded by crystal snifters on top of a nearby wooden cask. Several of the men helped themselves and sat back down. After a short time had passed, another group of men came down the stairs, followed by more of Sal's guys bringing up the rear, and brandishing weapons. This arriving group, of much younger men, about ten in all, and sporting the latest suits, were ushered over to where Sal and the others sat.

"Hey, we wuz told this wuz a party?" one of the men blurted, obviously upset, "and these guys took our guns, what's the deal?"

The Dons recognized that most of the individuals in this newly arrived group directly worked for them. They looked over at Sal and Nicky in confusion. "Hey Sal, what gives? Is this a-joke? These are our guys."

Sal re-crossed his short legs and motioned with a hand, again, to 'relax'. "We're still waitin' for one more guest," he said. After a few more minutes a lone, well-dressed man, arrived. He was the lieutenant of Tony Barbasonti, who turned towards Sal with surprise and asked, "Hey, what's he doin' here, Sal? What's goin' on?"

Sal motioned for the man who had just arrived to come closer.

Igino Costello walked forward and joined the group standing in front of the Dons. He shook a few reluctant hands before he addressed the men sitting, now in a half-circle, in front of him.

"Hey, Tony, what's the deal?" he asked his boss.

"I dunno, that's what we're all tryin' to figure out. Let's ask Sal and Nicky here," he pointed with a thumb. Everyone now turned their attention to Sal, who put his wine glass on the stone floor next to his chair, and then folded his hands over his vest.

"Boys," he began, "I suspect we all remember that Zhenobia broad and her guys who tried to pick a fight with us a few years ago?"

Everyone nodded and made subdued, colorful, comments. One said, "She still dead, right?" The others laughed, and Sal chuckled.

"Yeah, she's gone, but not the mooks she worked for," Sal replied.

"We imposed *Vendetta* on them crooks ... thought we got'm all?" another Don said.

Sal and Nicky nodded. "Yeah, we did ... mostly, but they're back, and now it's our business again," Nicky answered.

"Nick's right," Sal agreed, "we got a gang of foreign mooks tryin' to muscle in on our long haul trucking operation, and they're doin' it right under our noses, *capire?*"

The Dons moved uneasily in their seats at this news, some laughing in disbelief.

"Hey Sal, you gettin' paranoid in yer old age? Don't ya think we know what's goin' on in our business?" one replied.

The standing group, however, stood closer to each other as they looked nervously around.

"Sal, this is the first I'm hearin' about this, and it disturbs me. Who are these new guys?" One of the other Dons asked.

"These guys are called *la Mano Rossa,*" Sal replied.

Tommy Ceppelletti, one of the older Dons, now stood up. "I remember those guys from the old country. I thought they disappeared from over there, and so now you're tellin' us they're here, in our town?"

Sal and Nicky both nodded. "Yeah, Tommy, and these guys have been payin' off some of our people to ship they're stuff cross country, and then overseas from our docks. What'da yas think about that?"

There now was a great deal of commotion in the room, until Sal stood up and asked for quiet.

"Look, this is why I called yoos all here tonight, to figure this thing out, nice and quiet. Now, a few hours ago, the cops raided a big shipment of these trucks down at the port, arrested the drivers, and confiscated the trucks."

Again, the room got noisy. "I didn't hear anything about no raid?" several said.

"That's because you weren't supposed to," Sal loudly announced. "Like I was sayin,' this is happenin' right under our noses."

"How could this happen?" another of the Dons said angrily.

"Why don't yas ask your boys here?" Nicky answered, pointing his cane at the standing group of men. "Why don't ya ask Igino over there? How 'bout it, Igino, got somethin' to tell us, eh?"

The room got quiet as everyone turned to look at Igino Costello.

"Igino, what's he sayin'?" Tony Barbasonti said as he rose slowly from his chair.

Igino Costello licked his dry lips and looked nervously around for support. "Hey, Tony, c'mon, these guys got nothin' on us. Where's the proof, huh? I ain't sayin' nothin' …"

"You want proof?" Sal blustered, angrily, and pointing a finger at him, "I got proof for ya. Bring them guys in here," Sal ordered.

Several of Sal's men standing in back, holding shotguns, temporarily handed their weapons to their partners, and then quickly left. They returned a few minutes later, half-dragging, half-carrying, two men who looked as though they had been drug through a knothole. The handcuffed men were obviously prisoners. The guards brought the two forward and stood them before the Dons.

"Now," Sal began, "These two French mooks have been our guests for the last few hours. They work for the organization that is sponsoring the Red Hand gang in this country, and in our town, and they know who in our organization are the rats that have been selling us out under the table, don't ya boys?"

Both exhausted prisoners nodded.

"Good. Now be so kind as to point out who you been dealin' with, and payin' off," Sal told them.

"Him, the one you call, Igino," one of the prisoners replied in broken English.

Igino Costello, suddenly cursing a blue streak, quickly turned and tried to run, but found himself staring down the barrels of several shotguns held in the hands of Sal's men. Costello stopped abruptly and turned back around to face …

"What's this? What'ta you done, Igino?" Tony Barbasonti angrily asked, "I treat you like a son, give you responsibilities and authority, and you do this to me?"

"To us … to all of us," Sal corrected.

"Hey, Tony, ask him who else helped," Nicky interjected, "go ahead."

Tony came forward and stuck his face close to Igino's. "You tell us," he threatened, "you tell us now, *proprio adesso*, right now, *in fretta*."

"You keep yer trap shut, Igino," another member of those standing warned. Igino turned his head to the side to look at his guys. "It's over, they got us," he replied.

Then all bedlam broke loose as the standing ten broke into a confused, panic stricken, dead run for the stairs. But Sal's men had already formed a line of shotguns behind them. One of the rabbiting men reached down, pulled up one of his pant legs, and grabbed a berretta stuffed into the top of a stocking. But before he had the chance to use it, he was hit, along with a few others, by a blast of pellets from one of the shotguns. He fell to the floor, quite dead, while a few others of his comrades screamed in pain from flesh wounds.

"That's enough!" Sal shouted over the din and confusion. "Vin, Louie," Sal said behind him. The two holding submachine guns came forward and approached the six or seven who were still standing, and noisily pulled back the bolts of their respective weapons.

"Just say the word, Sal," Vinnie called out. The fleeing men all raised their hands and surrendered peacefully.

"Hey," Vinnie said to one of the men holding a shotgun, "I thought I told yas to make sure these punks had no toys?"

"Sorry, Vinni," came the reply.

"Now," Sal said, addressing the Dons, "we can mow these traitors down right here and now, or, you can take em home with you and do what you have to. But I'm tellin' ya, I don't wanna read in the papers about no more bodies floatin' around in the bay."

"More bodies? What'da yas mean, 'more bodies'?" another Don asked.

"What'sa matter? Ain't you been missin' Ralphy Lorenzo?" Sal asked, looking at each one.

"Ralphy? We heard he went to Italy."

"Nah," Sal replied, "we fished him, and his driver, outta the drink a day or so ago. They're parked in our freezer upstairs. Ralphy was up to his neck in this mess, just like Igino, and the rest of these mooks.

All the Dons looked at each other in amazement.

"Look, this is 'family business' and we should keep it that way, *capire?* The cops have nothin' to do with any of this, so let's not give 'em reason," Sal said, pointing with his thumb.

All the Dons nodded in agreement, and then made arrangements to take their delinquent people away. A few more hours passed and it was morning.

Simone Desaraux

Sal Canale sat in his office at the restaurant. He hadn't slept all night and he was feeling his age. Then his telephone rang. He sighed and picked up the receiver.

"Hello? ... Ah, *buongiorno,* so, how'd it go on your end, eh? ... Swell, same here, all cleaned up and we're hunting down any lose ends. These Red Hand punks should be outta commission real soon, you have my word. ... Yes, I understand your concern and we will be discreet, nothing to read about in the papers. ... Well, we all agreed that we got lazy. We need to police our own a little better so this thing won't happen again anytime soon. ... What? Is she alright? ... Did ya get that punk? ...Too bad ... Tell yas what, I'll have my guys put a hit out on him and ... Oh, okay if that's how ya wanna play it, good luck. ...Yeah, you too, Chief. See ya 'round. ... Yeah, *ciao.*

Sal Canale hung up the telephone, sat back, and wrung his face with one harry hand, wondering if it was all really over, or just beginning.

Chapter Twenty-Eight

Simone awoke in a hospital room with McCormick, along with a nurse, looking down at her.

"Welcome back, detective," McCormick smiled.

"What has happened to me? Did you catch him … Canard?" she asked with difficulty.

You need to rest, ma'am," the nurse replied. "I'll get the doctor," she said to McCormick, and then left.

"You're pretty banged up, but alive," McCormick answered. "And no, he still out there, but we'll get him as soon as you stop lying around her and are ready to get to work."

On hearing this, Simone tried to sit up on her own, but failed, until McCormick took her by her shoulders and gently pulled her up. Her head hurt and she discovered she had several strips of gauze bandages around her throat. Also, her left hand was wrapped thickly with bandages. She looked at her hand and wiggled her fingers.

"Glad you're ok," McCormick said.

"*Oui*, as am I. It was, how you say, 'a close one', for me," she replied, remembering. "And the rest of our team?"

"Recovered and back on duty," McCormick said.

"What was it they used on us, Mac ... the light and?"

McCormick pushed the hat back on his head. "I've experienced that once before, when Max and I first got real acquainted with these guys. It was some kinda grenade, I guess. Sure did the trick, alright. I'm just surprised that Canard had one."

"But we have concluded that he is in league with this *organisation du Cercle Noir* ..."

"Who?"

"Oh, forgive me, the Dark Circle," she corrected. "Obviously they have given him superior weapons to defend himself, yes?"

"Yeah," McCormick sadly replied, rubbing his eyes, "sure gonna make our job catching this guy harder."

"But not impossible. No, I refuse to accept defeat. Come, let us go ..." Simone said as she pushed the sheet off her and threw her legs over the side of the bed.

"Wait a minute, young woman," a man's voice from behind them said. McCormick turned and saw the doctor enter the room flanked by a nurse, "and where do you think you're going?"

"*Monsieur le docteur*, I am leaving to catch a murder," Simone replied as her feet hit the floor.

"Oh really? Dressed like that?" the doctor said with a smirk.

The nurse put her hand to her mouth to suppress a giggle and McCormick respectfully turned his back. Simone unwittingly stood before them clad in only her undergarments.

"*Mon Dior,*" she exclaimed as she tore the top sheet off the bed and quickly covered herself with it. "Where are my *vêtements?*"

"Excuse me?" the doctor asked.

Simone sighed angrily, "My clothes, what have you done with them?"

"They were bloodstained and torn," the nurse answered, "here, let me get you a robe," she offered, going to a closet in the room, taking out a white hospital robe, and assisted her putting it on.

"*Mes chaussures, s'il vous plait,*" Simone rattled off.

The nurse wrinkled up her forehead.

"My shoes," Simone translated, visibly annoyed.

"I'm sorry, ma'am, you only came in with one," the nurse apologized.

Simone spewed out a string of French verbiage that sounded remarkably like cursing. McCormick now turned back around and said. "Take it easy, detective. As soon as we can get you outta here, we can go to my house where your stuff is and you'll be ready to hit the streets …"

"When I release her, you mean," the doctor corrected.

"Oh yeah, sure doc," McCormick agreed.

"Now then, young woman, let's have a look at you, shall we?"

An hour or so later McCormick, along with Simone, pulled up in front of the McCormick home. McCormick got out and took a quick look around, before the two went inside. Maxine was sitting in an overstuffed chair reading and drinking tea, while a police detective sat in the back of the room with a shotgun resting on his lap. McCormick nodded to him as they entered. Maxine looked up and smiled.

"Well, it's about time you two came home. I was about to bust outta here and form a search party," she said, half-jokingly.

"Sorry sweetheart, long night," McCormick said, coming over and kissing her. Afterward, Maxine looked over at Simone, dressed in a hospital robe, and wearing McCormick's trench coat over her shoulders.

"Long night, huh? I'll bet," Maxine wise-cracked.

"Now, Max, it ain't what it looks like …" McCormick began to explain. Simone took off the coat and laid it on the sofa. That's when Maxine saw the bandages on her hand and neck.

"Simone, you're hurt, what happened? Mac, what happened?" Maxine insisted and tried to get up.

"Hey, you just relax, will ya," McCormick said, gently pushing her back down.

"*Oui,* Maxine, please ... it is nothing, I assure you. Allow me to go to my room and dress and then your husband and I will tell you what happened, A-OK?"

Maxine smiled, "A-Okay, Simone. I'll wait right here."

"*Bon,* I will be right back," Simone said as she headed for the stairs in the back of the room.

When she was gone, Maxine looked up at her husband with concern. "Is she A-Okay, Mac?

McCormick removed his hat, and then sat heavily down in the chair across from her. "Yeah, but it was a close one, for sure," he replied quietly.

"How close?" Maxine asked.

"That Canard clown had her in his clutches. She would've been done for if we hadn't showed up when we did. We really gotta get this guy, Max," he sighed.

"What about that other gang ... the Red Hand?"

"Gone for the time being. Sal and his boys are seeing to that."

Maxine chuckled, "I'll just bet they are. Now, how about our other friends?" she inquired more seriously.

"Max, we caught a couple of their guys, and they were helpful, but I dunno how big of a black eye we gave their organization. I guess we'll find out down the road."

Maxine, stared past McCormick for a long time, until …

"Max, you alright?" McCormick asked, leaning forward.

Maxine snapped out of it. "Oh, yeah, sorry darling … it's nothing, really."

"Yeah, and that's what worries me," McCormick replied with concern.

"Alright, look, it's just a matter of time before they try something else, or just plain come after us. I just hope we're ready when it happens," Maxine said, putting both hands on her belly.

McCormick got up, kneeled next to her, and placed his hands on top of hers.

"Hey, whatever happens, we're a family and we'll handle it as a family, okay?"

Maxine smiled, and then leaned over to kiss him, long and deep. Then someone in the room cleared there throat slightly. Simone stood there in a snappy grey business suit and heels.

"*Excusez-moi,* I do not mean to interrupt, but we have much to accomplish, yes?" she asked, looking at McCormick.

"You two kids run along. I'm comfy right here," Maxine said, giving her husband a quick wink.

McCormick got up, pecked his wife on the cheek, and then went over to Simone. "Ok, detective, let's hit the road," he said.

As they left, McCormick stopped briefly to check with Maxine's body guard, compliments of Chief Clifford, and then they left, driving directly to police headquarters for debriefing.

Chapter Twenty-Nine

"Quite'a night," Clifford said; as he lounged behind his desk, sipping on a cup of coffee. McCormick and Simone sat in familiar chairs in front of Clifford's desk and waited. Clifford then went on to explain, in detail, the raid on the warehouse. "And we arrested a captain and some of his crew before they tried to weigh anchor. Seems like a couple of the truck drivers figured it would help their case with the D.A. by volunteering which boat in port was their shipment's ride overseas."

"Congratulations, Chief," McCormick said, leaning back and yawning.

"Looks like you could use about eight hours, McCormick," Clifford observed.

"Yeah, I'll sleep like a baby when this is over," McCormick replied.

"Yeah, you and me both."

Clifford now looked directly at Simone. "So, Detective Desaraux, how're you feeling?" he asked, pointing to her bandaged hand and throat, "the doctor called me from the hospital and said you were fit for light duty. How do you feel about that?"

Simone stood up at attention. "Sir, I am ready to continue with my investigation and capture of the criminal Andre Canard, with the help of detective Mac, of course," she replied, and almost saluted.

Clifford worked his jaw and then motioned for her to sit. He put his coffee mug down and leaned forward, placing both arms on his paper strewn desktop.

"Detective, I want you to listen carefully," Clifford began, "you had an awful close call last night ... to close for comfort as far as I'm concerned. If it hadn't been for McCormick and the other cops, well, you'd be on a slab in our morgue right now, missing an ear. Mac filled me in about what happened in that house, and in that park, while you were unconscious in the emergency room. Now, I just got a telegram from a Chief Inspector Jean Pierre Russo, he's your boss, right? Well, he's worried about you, and quite frankly, so am I. Now, he said that if I felt that you were in mortal danger, to put you on the first flight back to France. I'm considering this right now ..."

Simone abruptly stood up again, "*Je vous demande pardon, monsieur,* I mean, excuse me, Chief, but we are so close to catching this beast ... if you will allow me to continue my pursuit of ..."

"*Our* pursuit, detective," Clifford strongly corrected, and jabbing a finger at her, "*our* case, *our* resources. This guy's murdered in *our* city, so as of right now, he's *our* responsibility to bring him to justice and to trial *here*, in the U.S. Now, the higher-ups in both departments can wrangle over international law, extradition, and whatever else, but for right now, Andre Canard is *our* manhunt. Are we clear, detective?"

Simone sighed heavily and plopped back down. McCormick remained silent as he chewed on the inside of his cheek.

"Look, detective," Clifford continued, "you've done an outstanding job since you've been here, and as far as I'm concerned, if you were one of my people, we wouldn't be havin' this conversation right now ... you'd be hittin' the streets lookin' for this guy ... but you're not. You're a visiting foreign national with no peace officer status in this country. Matter of fact, you're not even supposed to be carrying a weapon, officially, but I've allowed it, and a good thing, right McCormick?"

McCormick nodded in agreement. "You'll get no argument from me, boss," he replied and then winked over at Simone.

Simone smiled briefly in acknowledgement.

"However," Clifford continued, "the way things are, and the way your boss feels, and how *my* boss feels, especially after last night, if anything serious, or fatal happens to you, it'll become an international departmental incident ..."

"Is that your concern, Chief, the paperwork? Or is it because I am a woman?" Simone fired back.

"No, it's shipping your mutilated body back across the ocean. That's *all* of our concern, detective," Clifford barked.

"Take it easy, Chief," McCormick said, "she ain't dead."

"Yet," he blustered. "Look, you two, I'm caught in the middle of this, between a rock and a hard place ..."

Simone looked at McCormick, wrinkling up her forehead. McCormick gestured the 'never mind' sign as Clifford plowed on, unabated.

"... So, that being said, and all things considered, my decision is that you, detective, from this moment on, are officially off the streets as far as this case is concerned. However, you will be retained on this continent, for the time being, in an advisory capacity only, understand?"

Simone just sat there; working her jaw, with both hands folded in her lap, and nodding.

"And so, I am to be a *consultante* only, *oui?*" she said quietly.

"If that's means we only need you for additional information on this guy, yes, that's it. Any questions? Clifford asked.

"No, sir," Simone replied tightly.

"Good. Now lemme suggest that you go home and get some sleep, you've earned it. Maybe McCormick can give you a lift back to the house ... and then I need you back in here, Mac, as soon as you can," Clifford said, ending the discussion.

"No problem, Chief. C'mon detective, let's take you home," McCormick said, standing up.

Simone mechanically nodded and stood up. Then she took a deep breath, snapped to attention, stomped her right foot hard on the floor, and expertly saluted Clifford. Clifford cleared his throat, lowered his gaze momentarily, then without objection, stood, and returned the salute. "Thank you for your service," he said to her.

"*Merci,*" Simone replied, then turned on her heel and left the office.

McCormick and Clifford looked at each other and shook their heads with mutual understanding, and then McCormick followed Simone out the door.

Chapter Thirty

"Well, you two are back early," Maxine said as she exited the kitchen holding a dinner plate with a sandwich in one hand and a glass of cold milk in the other. She maneuvered over to the patrolman who sat in the back of the large parlor with a loaded shotgun lying across his lap. She handed him the food and asked if he needed anything else.

"No he doesn't," McCormick replied for him from the doorway.

The patrolman put the food down on the floor next to him, stood up, and saluted.

"Knock that off. I'm a P.I.," McCormick corrected.

"Not according to Chief Clifford, sir, he was real clear about that," the cop nervously replied.

"Alright, officer, just make sure that my wife knows whoever walks into this room, if she doesn't, shoot, ya got that?"

"Yes, sir, detective," the cop saluted again.

"And knock that off," McCormick complained as Simone slid past him and sat down.

Maxine put a hand on her hip and tipped her head to one side. McCormick got the message and said to the cop, "And enjoy your sandwich. Max, I gotta go back to the office."

Maxine pointed to the food on the floor and then to the policeman. He smiled, picked it up, and dove in. Maxine went over to her husband and gave him a quick kiss. Then they both looked over at Simone who was just sitting on a sofa and staring down at her bandaged hand.

"Alright, what happened?" Maxine asked in a whisper, looking up at McCormick.

"Politics," he said, shaking his head.

"Oh really? Just spill it," she said tapping a toe.

McCormick rolled his eyes and gave her a quick rundown.

"So, she grounded?" Maxine said.

"Looks that way, sweetheart. Hey, I gotta get back, see you tonight," McCormick said, and turned to leave.

"Hang on a second, buster, did you forget?"

"Forget what?"

"I gotta doctor's appointment in about an hour,"

"Have the cop back there take you," McCormick replied, and pointing with a thumb.

"He doesn't have'a car; they dropped him off when they changed shifts."

"Well, I'll call the precinct and have 'em send over a black and white to take you."

Maxine sighed and shook her head. "Why don't you have them pick *you* up, and take *you* downtown, and you leave me the Caddy?"

"How 'bout I call a taxi for ya?" McCormick countered.

"Mac, do you know how long it takes a cab to get here? And besides, do you know how many germs there are in those back seats … and quite frankly a squad car isn't much better …" Maxine carried on.

McCormick held up both hands in surrender. "Ok, ok, you've made your point. Take the Caddy," he replied, handing her the keys. "Hey, wait a second, can you still fit behind the wheel?"

"Well, yeah ... I think," Maxine said, looking down at her protruding belly at different angles. "I'll just jack the seat back real good," she smiled.

McCormick crossed his arms over his chest. "How 'bout your feet reaching the pedals?"

Maxine face reddened up like a firecracker. "Hey, ya big lug, I can't help it if I'm short," she retorted, and punched him in the arm.

"I will drive her, if it is permitted," Simone replied from the sofa.

Maxine looked at her husband with a big smile. "Yeah, what a great idea. Thanks Simone."

"*Aucun problem,*" Simone replied, smiling back.

Maxine rattled off a few sentences of appreciation in fluid French, until McCormick held up a hand.

"Hold on, Simone, do have a driver's license?"

"*Certainement je,* for a very long time," she replied.

"Mac, stuff'a sock in it and go to work, will ya? Us girls will be fine. Now go use the phone," Maxine mildly scolded.

McCormick shook his head and went to make the call. A few minutes later, a squad car pulled up in front of the house and blew the horn.

"Alright, I'm outta here," McCormick said, coming over and giving Maxine a farewell kiss. "Lemme know how junior is will ya?"

"You mean our daughter, don't ya?" Maxine smiled up into his face.

"Yeah, right," he replied, kissing her one more time. "Oh, by the way," he said, remembering something and turning to Simone. He reached into an outside pocket and retrieved Simone's Walther P38, and handed it to her. "Ya prolly won't need this, but it's your property and I'm tired of carrying it around," McCormick grinned.

"*Merci, Mac,*" she replied, taking the weapon, checking the clip, and then sliding it behind her back under her suit jacket.

The car horn sounded again, prompting McCormick to say, "I gotta go, see yas." And he was out of the room, down the hall, and through the front door.

Maxine turned to Simone and smiled mischievously at her. "After my appointment, we're going shopping, my treat," she said, squeezing Simone's good arm. Simone politely laughed and nodded. "How's the hand? Maxine asked.

"Just a deep cut, but no permanent damage," Simone replied, holding the bandaged hand up.

"Good, but just in case, go into the kitchen and you'll find a pot of tea on the stove. Help yourself; there are cups in the cupboard. I'm gonna go get dressed. Be right back," Maxine said, as she waddled away.

Simone did just that, and, after drinking down the first cup, she immediately felt refreshed and invigorated. "I must ask Maxine what kind of tea this is," she said, pouring herself a second cup.

Chapter Thirty-One

It was a pleasant drive from the suburbs into the city for Maxine's appointment. They arrived in plenty of time giving Maxine and Simone the opportunity to chat away in Simone's native tongue to the chagrin and irritation of several other expectant mothers in the waiting room. Finally, it was Maxine's turn with the doctor, leaving Simone to sit alone and read a magazine. After a while Maxine returned, giving Simone the 'thumbs up' gesture that everything was just fine with her pregnancy.

"So, let's get some food and then hit the stores," Maxine said, as the two women left the office. They found a nice restaurant to enjoy a late lunch. Simone was amazed how much food Maxine could put away in one sitting.

"Hey, I'm eatin' for two," she laughed. Afterward, they re-parked the car and went window shopping. Maxine picked out some nice American outfits for Simone and insisted that she try them on. Several were purchased, compliments of the McCormicks.

Simone was very flattered by Maxine's generosity and companionship, and the two quickly became fast friends. It was just beginning to be evening when the two exited the last clothing store, laden down with shopping bags. After putting their cargo in the trunk, they both got in and prepared for the ride home.

"Gosh, my dogs are barkin'," Maxine complained, kicking off her shoes.

"I am sorry, Maxine, but I do not hear *les aboiements de chiens,*" Simone replied, looking around outside.

"Maxine laughed out loud and explained the term as she held up a foot.

Simone joined her in shared laughter to the point that tears began to run down their faces. That's when a car pulled up alongside of them. Simone casually looked over and ... "My God, Maxine, get down!" she screamed as Simone's side window exploded, sending glass chips flying everywhere. Simone quickly reached behind her back and pulled her weapon, but by the time she sat up, the auto peeled away.

"Are you wounded?" Simone asked, Maxine.

"Nah. So, what'da ya waitin' for? Go get 'em," Maxine hollered.

Simone started the car and stepped on the accelerator. The Caddy launched forward, pushing the two back in the seat.

"It was him," Simone said, as she drove in hot pursuit, trying to shorten the distance between them.

"Who?" Maxine yelled, trying to hold on.

"Canard, the beast," Simone replied, taking a corner hard and sending Maxine into the door. "I am sorry, your *bébé,* maybe we should just call it in and ..."

"Don't you dare, sister," Maxine shouted back, "this kid's a McCormick and it better get used to villains, bullets, and car chases. No time like the present to learn, so step on it."

And Simone did. They chased the car down side streets and out of the downtown area.

"Looks like they're heading for the railway yards," Maxine grunted as the car bounced and swayed around obstacles and trash cans that the other car in front of them was hitting. After another mile, the car they were chasing made a hard left, turning down a washed out side road that went under a highway overpass and ran along what appeared to be an abandoned rail line. Then it swerved to a stop in a swirl of dust and gravel. On seeing this, Simone put the brakes on hard as the Caddy came to a sliding halt a few yards away. Simone checked her weapon before she said, "Stay here," to Maxine.

"Oh, baloney on that," Maxine replied as she reached into her pocketbook and pulled out a Smith and Wesson .45.

Suddenly, the rear window of the Caddy was completely blown inward by what sounded like a shotgun blast. Both women covered their faces and eyes from the flying glass and pellets. Then Maxine's door was flung open, and a man's hand reached in, grabbed a fist full of auburn hair, and pulled Maxine out of her side of the vehicle.

"Maxine!" Simone yelled, as she attempted to grab a foot, but too late ...

"Step out of the car, detective, or I will gut this woman," a man's voice boomed with a French accent.

Simone swallowed hard and got out. When she slowly walked around the front of the car she saw Maxine being held by an unidentified man, who was holding a knife under Maxine's throat.

"*Perdre le fusil.* Lose the gun," he ordered.

Simone dropped her weapon where she stood and walked forward towards them.

"*Arrêtez!* Stop," the assailant said, pushing the knife blade into Maxine's neck.

"Let her go, she is innocent," Simone pleaded.

"Unlikely," the man replied.

"Who are you? What do you want with us?" Simone asked.

"I want nothing from either of you," he replied grimly, "however, there is someone who has *inachevé* ... unfinished business with you, *détective*," he said, turning his head in the direction of the other car and nodding.

Simone heard a car door slam. When she looked over at the auto the two women were chasing, she saw a man walking towards them.

"Andre Canard," she whispered, trying not to panic.

Canard casually came forward, smoking a cigarette as if he were on an evening stroll. The sun was just beginning to set behind the water tower of the railway yard, making the shadows long and everything seem surreal. When Canard was a few feet away, he stopped dropped his spent cigarette on the ground, and then slowly crushed it with the toe of his patent leather shoe.

"*Monsieur,* shall I dispose of this woman," the man holding Maxine asked.

Canard, didn't reply at first, he just reached into an outside pocket of his long coat and retrieved a pair of black leather gloves and began to put them on.

"Spare this woman," Simone asked, trying to keep her panic in check, and you can do what you will to me."

"I will do what I will with you regardless," Canard replied smoothly, without emotion.

"So, you must be the French idiot, along with your mutt here, who my husband is gonna catch real soon and put into the electric chair. Hope ya like the smell of roast pig," Maxine courageously spat.

The two men laughed at the futile attempt of Maxine's impertinence.

"*Pierre, ferme sa bouche.* Pierre, shut her mouth, but keep her alive. I don't believe I have had the pleasure of strangling a woman that is with child. It might be amusing for me."

"No!" Simone screamed, as Pierre, struck Maxine on the head with the handle of his knife. Maxine crumpled to her knees, dazed by the blow.

"Now, détective, it is time for you to go to join your papa," Canard threatened, as a garroting wire appeared in his gloved hands. Then he rushed towards her. Simone put up two fists and prepared to defend herself, when, suddenly, they all heard a gunshot. Both Canard and Simone looked around, but saw no one else. Pierre, on the other hand, audibly grunted, letting go of Maxine who fell onto her side.

"Pierre?" Canard said. But Pierre was no longer listening, as the front of his outer jacket turned crimson. He looked straight past Canard, took two steps forward, and fell heavily onto the ground.

"Pierre!" Canard shouted, discarding the wire, reaching into another pocket, and pulling out a gun.

Another concussion rang out, closer now, giving Simone the opportunity to rush over to assist the fallen Maxine. Canard screamed with rage as he clutched his now punctured gun hand, the weapon flying uselessly out of his grip.

"Maxine?" Simone anxiously said, as she leaned over her. It was at that moment that a human shadow appeared seemingly out of nowhere. It effortlessly leaped over the two women, and the dead man, and attack Canard with such precision that the Frenchman simply had no defense. The shadow made short work of Canard, incapacitating him by breaking both of his arms, and sending him, helplessly, to his knees. Canard sat on his haunches, gasping in pain before the two women. Then the shadow strode over to the front of the Caddy, picked up Simone's gun, walked over to her, and held it out.

"Finish him," the shadow ordered with a woman's voice. Simone, hesitated, not really sure what to do.

"Take it," the woman ordered again.

Simone cautiously accepted the weapon and stood up.

"Who are you?" Simone asked the shadow who was, except for the eyes, completely covered in tight black silk from head to toe.

"No one of concern to you. Now, do what you came here to do, finish him. It is my gift," she replied.

"Don't do it, Simone, or you'll be just like him," Maxine interrupted, as she pushed herself upright to a sitting position, "Don't sell your soul. You're a cop, remember? Like your father."

Simone looked at the Walther in her hand, and then at Canard, sitting on his legs a few feet away from her. Simone swallowed, walked over and stood before him. She raised her weapon and pointed it straight at his head. Canard looked up and smiled, wickedly, at her.

"Go ahead, *chérie,* send me to hell."

Simone started to squeeze the trigger ... but then stopped. She sighed heavily, sucked back some tears, blinked several times, and moved the gun away.

"Andrea Canard, I arrest you for murder in the name of the law," she finally said to him.

Suddenly, from behind, Simone felt her shoulder, just below her neck, being squeezed. She involuntarily dropped the gun, and felt her legs strangely unable to support her. She wobbled momentarily, and then joined Canard on the ground.

"Sorry, that's not the arrangement," the shadow woman said. Without another word, she stepped around Simone and retrieved the garroting wire that Canard had discarded. Then she stood behind Canard and wrapped the garrote around his neck. It was quick, final, and without mercy. All Simone could do was squat there and watch. Then a short, oriental looking, blade appeared in the shadow's hand which she used to skillfully remove Canard's right ear. After the knife disappeared, the ear was wrapped in a piece of black cloth and shoved into a fold in her outfit. The shadow woman then turned and began to walk away.

Simone Desaraux sat on her legs, breathing heavily, and looking at the dead body of the mass murderer, Andre Canard, who lie in front of her, mangled and bleeding. Simone closed her eyes and tried to control her emotions, and her thoughts. It was over now. She could return home.

"Simone, you ok?" Maxine asked from behind her.

Simone turned her head to the side and replied, "*Oui*, A-OK,"

"Well, I'm not."

Simone, with some effort, managed to stagger to her feet and steady herself, she looked down at the body one more time, spit on it, said "*Cochon*", and then went over to where Maxine was sitting on the ground.

"Can ya give a gal a-hand up," Maxine asked.

Simone helped her to her feet ... And that's when it happened. Maxine's water broke.

"Oh my God. Here? You wanna be born here?" Maxine shouted at her belly.

"*Mon Dieu, Maxine,* we must get you to *l'hôpital,*" Simone said anxiously, helping her towards the Caddy.

Maxine groaned in pain as the first contraction hit her.

"It ain't gonna happen, Simone, this kid is comin' fast," Maxine groaned and puffed.

"Let us get you into the auto," Simone urged.

"Wait," Maxine objected, "too much glass, it's all over the place. Let's get to the other car, hurry," she panted.

Simone put Maxine's arm around her neck and the two hobbled over to Canard's vehicle. Simone opened the rear passenger door, and helped Maxine lay down on the back seat. Maxine pulled her dress up and told Simone to pull off her drawers. Simone did so and gasped.

"Maxine, the *bébé* is coming," she exclaimed.

Maxine was puffing like a locomotive, "Yep, she's comin' down the shoot ... Mac, where are you?" she cried out. "Simone, have you ever delivered a kid before?" Maxine asked between contractions.

"Only in training at the academy, but they were *mannequins*," Simone replied wide-eyed with apprehension.

"Dummies, huh?" Maxine laughed as she puffed and groaned some more, "Well, welcome to my world, sweetheart." Then she cried out as another contraction hit her.

Simone looked away for just a moment and noticed the shadow woman standing off in the distanced, slinging a scoped rifle over her shoulder.

"Hey! *Madame.* Call for help. Get help." Simone shouted at her.

The black clad woman simply turned and walked away, leaving Simone and Maxine completely alone. Simone cursed savagely, but then turned her attention back to Maxine and the challenge at hand.

"Hey, look, Simone," Maxine said, drenched with sweat, and trying to sit up on her elbows, "just hang in there, it shouldn't be long."

"*Oui*, I am here for you, Maxine, I will not leave," she replied, taking off her jacket and rolling up the sleeves of her blouse.

Maxine screamed from her very depths, one last time, the sound echoing off the surrounding trees and concrete, as the final birth pangs struck with all their fury.

"It is coming, Maxine ... I see the head ... Push Maxine, *pousser, pousser* ..." Simone urged.

A moment later the sounds of birth pangs were replaced by the crying of a new life, as Simone held up a baby girl in front of Maxine.

"*Félicitations, Maxine,* how wonderful," Simone exclaimed, as she gently placed the child into Maxine's waiting arms. Maxine cradled her baby as tears ran down her cheeks in rivulets.

"I can't believe it, I just can't believe it," Maxine kept repeating as she tenderly kissed her baby's small forehead.

Simone just stood there, mesmerized, framed by the rear passenger door like a silhouette in the rising moonlight, her knees resting on the back seat. She wept freely, not only because of the new life she had just helped bring into the world, but also because she now heard sirens wailing in the distance ... and they were getting closer.

Chapter Thirty-Two

The new parents smiled happily for the variety of cameramen and reporters that were wedged into a private hospital room. The couples photos were repeatedly taken while over eager reporters plied them with questions, anxious to know more details, regarding the case of the French mass murderer, Andre Canard, and Maxine McCormick's narrow escape from certain death, causing the premature birth of her daughter.

Maxine sat up in her hospital bed, surrounded by multiple bouquets of flowers, as she cradled the new baby girl in her arms. Earlier, both had been cleaned up, examined thoroughly, fed, and well rested, before McCormick, Chief of Police Clifford, and hospital medical staff, allowed any visitors to enter the room, especially members of the press. McCormick, dressed in his best suit, stood alongside his wife, smiling, nodding in appreciation, and shaking a few hands.

On the other side of the bed stood Chief Clifford and Detective Simone Desaraux, who were both receiving congratulations on bringing down a dangerous criminal, along with the gang he was affiliated with, thus making the city streets safe again. Also in the room was the incumbent District Attorney, along with the Deputy Mayor. Neither city officials were wasting the opportunity to do what politicians do, especially during an election year.

"I just want to formally reiterate to the members of our city's newspapers, that his Honor the Mayor, along with myself, the District Attorney as well as the Police Commissioner, are so proud of the Metropolitan Police Department and its outstanding job in bringing to a close this latest criminal investigation. I would also like to personally thank Chief of Police, Clifford, along with those brave souls whom the department deems fit to employ as consultants, such as ex-police detective, Shawn McCormick, who is no stranger to high praise from this office for past contributions to the welfare of this city. The Mayor would also like to thank the department for their outstanding job of coordinating with French police authorities, along with their liaison, Detective Simone Desaraux, in ridding our streets, as well as those of Paris, of the mass killer, Andre Canard, whose body lies in our city's morgue. The result also being, I'm informed, the removal of a notorious gang called the Red Hand, that this criminal Canard was a part of. Now, I would be remiss in my duty, both civically and morally, if I did not give due praise to Detective McCormick's wife, Mrs. Maxine McCormick, for her outstanding bravery under fire, resulting in the miraculous birth, under dire circumstances, of their new daughter. I must say, that with the caliber of civic minded people like these, working in our behalf, we can, without any doubt, feel secure in our city. Thank you all for your service and your bravery."

The deputy mayor now turned and began to applaud prompting everyone else of the press corps to followed suit ... And that's when the baby woke up. On that note, hospital staff ushered everyone out of the room, except McCormick, Clifford and Simone. Once the door was closed, drapes were pulled around Maxine's hospital bed so she could nurse in private.

Clifford now pulled McCormick and Simone to the other side of the room.

"Sorry for the circus you two, but it's an election year," Clifford said as quietly as he could.

"No worries, Chief ... all part of the job," McCormick replied.

Clifford stuck his hand out and the two men shook.

"Congratulations, Mac, you're a daddy now. How does it feel?"

McCormick rubbed his face with a large hand. "I honestly dunno. I haven't gotten used to the idea yet. I thought I had another month or so to prepare," he replied.

"Nature waits for no one," Simone replied.

"Picked out a name, yet?" Clifford asked.

"Nah, well, we were kicking a few around, but haven't settled on anything …"

"Yes we have," Maxine said from behind the curtain.

McCormick rolled both eyes and pointed to his ears.

"Yeah, Mac, I hear real good. I'm finished now, you guys can come back.

The three walked over and McCormick pulled back the drapes. Maxine lay there, propped up by two pillows holding the baby who was sleeping soundly as she gently stroked her head.

"You were sayin', sweetheart?" McCormick replied leading over and kissing Maxine and the baby.

"Well, we did discuss quite a few names, but ... well, to be honest, when I was in that thugs grip, a name popped into my head," she replied.

"Yer kiddin'?" McCormick said.

Maxine looked up at him and shook her head.

"So what is it?" Clifford asked.

"Mac, how about, Victoria Rose McCormick? We can just call her, Rose. Wha'da ya think?"

McCormick put both hands into his pockets, put his head down and thought ... then he paced back and forth a few times, but said, nothing.

"Mac?" Maxine said, looking over at the other two for support.

"Fer cryin' out loud, McCormick, say something, before I put my foot down and name my Goddaughter, Dewy," Clifford threatened.

McCormick halted in mid-stride, turned and looked at his wife. Then he smiled widely, "Sweetheart, I like it. Rose it is," he said. Maxine began to cry as she held out a free hand. McCormick went over and the couple embraced. "Victoria Rose, that's a swell name," he whispered into her ear.

Clifford rocked back and forth on his heels and chuckled, while Simone dabbed away tears with a lace handkerchief.

"Well, I'm glad that's settled," Clifford signed. "Now, I'm not sure if this is the best time for this," he began by first looking over at the closed room door before continuing, "but I'm curious about this mysterious person that Simone was tellin' me about, that showed up and saved your lives."

"It was a woman," Simone said.

"Yeah, a real dragon lady ... and she had some serious skills. If I didn't know better, I'd almost say Zhenobia had returned from the grave," Maxine added.

"I haven't heard about this," McCormick said, coming over to them.

"You were busy becoming a father, Mac, and Maxine there had just been through quite an experience ... figured you had enough on your plate. By the way, Max, how's the head?" Clifford asked, pointing to his own head.

Maxine tapped lightly on her skull with her knuckles. "Hard as Gibraltar, Chief," she laughed.

"Yeah, good thing," McCormick sighed, looking over at her. Maxine winked back, and then gently moved Rose to a different arm.

"This *femme mystère,* this mystery woman, killed Andre Canard's partner with a single shot, and did so from a distance, in the dark, while he was holding onto Maxine ... an amazing feat," Simone said.

"And then she shot the gun outta Canard's hand. After that, she was on him like-a bad smell," Maxine finished.

"Yeah, I got a quick preliminary report from the coroner," Clifford said, "seems he was busted up pretty bad, and his head was just about taken off. Any idea who this woman might be?"

McCormick and Maxine looked with understanding at each other.

"Sounds like the Dark Circle is cleaning up loose ends," McCormick answered. Maxine nodded.

"She's an assassin, an agent, like Zhenobia was," Maxine added, "I can't help but wonder, though, why she didn't finish Simone and me off?"

"Perhaps it had something to do with what she said to me when I decided not to accept her offer, her 'gift', as she put it, to kill Canard, but instead I decided to arrest him."

Simone when on to explain the details of the whole encounter, and the execution of Canard.

"So what'd she say?" McCormick asked.

"She said that Canard's arrest was not the arrangement ... and then she disabled me and killed him.

No one said anything for a few long moments, until ...

"She was sent specifically to kill Canard and his mutt, not us ... at least not this time anyway," Maxine concluded.

"Or, next time either as far as I'm concerned," Clifford said.

McCormick said nothing, but quietly went back over to sit next to his wife and baby.

Chapter Thirty-Three

Several more days passed until Maxine and Rose were given a clean bill of health and allowed to go home, amid the clatter and drop cloths of workmen fixing bullet riddled walls, ruined doors, and replacing damaged furniture, all on the tab of the city, courtesy of City Hall.

Simone spent a few more days with the McCormick's and their new baby, until another telegram was received from Paris summoning her home immediately. And so Simone Desaraux stood at the door of the McCormick home, suitcase next to her feet, and holding Victoria Rose McCormick in her arms. After a few last kisses and some tears, Simone handed her back to Maxine, who gave her to McCormick so she could embrace Simone and speak words of gratitude to her again for what she had done.

"*Vous me manquerez tous les deux,*" Simone said, wiping away a stray tear.

"And we will miss you too, Simone," Maxine said. "Please come and visit anytime."

"*Merci,*" Simone replied, eyes glistening in the morning sunlight.

McCormick stuck out a free hand and they shook. "Safe flight, partner, and be careful over there," McCormick said.

Simone nodded. Just then a yellow taxi pulled up to the curb in front of the house and tooted its horn.

"Well, I guess I must go," Simone said, picking up her suitcase.

"Here, lemme give ya a hand with that," McCormick said, handing the baby back to Maxine, and taking the suitcase from Simone.

"*Merci*, Mac, but unnecessary ..."

"No, it isn't," McCormick insisted, and walked past her off the porch and towards the waiting cab. Maxine gave her one last hug and then Simone turned and followed McCormick.

Suddenly, half-dozen police squad cars pulled around the corner, with their lights flashing, and stopped in front of the McCormick home. They were followed by a private car that pulled up behind them. Chief Clifford got out and waved his arm at the other cars. The officers inside all got out, dressed in full dress uniforms, and formed a neat line on the sidewalk. Clifford, also dressed in formal blue, went over and dismissed the taxi. Then he stood in front of the line of officers. He motioned for Simone to step forward. Simone looked at McCormick and wrinkled her forehead. McCormick smiled and nodded at her. Simone cleared her throat and went over and stood in front of Chief Clifford. Clifford shouted, "Attention!" The line of officers snapped to attention. Clifford removed his cap, and stepped up close to Simone. He had a rectangular box under his left arm. After clearing his throat, he spoke.

"Detective, First Class, Simone Antoinette Desaraux ..."

"*Excusie Moi*, Chief, but I am not a *détective* first class ..."

Clifford cleared his throat, again, loudly, "Well you are now, according to your Chief, and as of this morning. Now, stand there and don't interrupt me"

Simone stood at attention. "*Oui*, Boss."

"Detective Desaraux, on behalf of the City, the Mayor, the Metropolitan Police Department, the Police Commissioner, and myself, I present you with the Police Departments Medal of Valor," Clifford announced, opening the box, handing it to Simone, and then pinning the medal on her jacket. Then Clifford took one step back and saluted, as did the rest of the police officers. Simone cried freely and saluted back. Afterward everyone applauded. Clifford stepped up to her and planted a kiss on both cheeks. "I understand this is customary?" he said.

Simone couldn't stop smiling. "*Oui*, boss. *Merci beaucoup.*"

"Now, we're going to escort you, with full honors, to the airport. McCormick, put her bag in the back of my car. Detective, you ride shotgun," Clifford said as he made a circular motion with his arm prompting the officers to quickly get into their squad cars.

Simone looked at McCormick with a wrinkled forehead and mouthed, "Shotgun?"

McCormick, Clifford and Simone walked over to Clifford's new Buick.

"New car, Chief?" McCormick asked as he placed the suitcase into the back seat.

"Yeah it is, and don't ask to borrow it, either," Clifford politely growled. "Your Caddy's being overhauled as we speak," he said as he held the passenger door open for Simone. Once she was inside, Clifford came around and slid into the driver's seat. Then he rolled down his side window.

"Take it easy, Mac, I'll call ya later," Clifford said. Simone leaned forward. *"Au revoir,* Mac, I will miss you."

McCormick nodded, gave her a quick wink, and then stood back. Clifford blew his horn and the line of squad cars forming the escort to the airport, three in front and three behind, left the curb, sirens blaring, and headed down the street. McCormick waited until they were out of sight before returning to Maxine and Rose on the front porch. Maxine was crying softly, while Rose was asleep in her arms.

"I'm gonna miss her, Mac. She's quite the woman," Maxine said.

"Yeah, she is, but so are you, cupcake," McCormick replied, looking over at her. Maxine smiled warmly, tipped her head back as McCormick kissed her deeply ... That is until they heard a sharp crash from behind them and someone complain, "Hey! Keep it down you guys; these folks have'a new baby."

The McCormick's smiled at each other, turned, and went inside the house.

Simone Desaraux

Chapter Thirty-Four

Simone sat quietly in her first class seat, compliments of Chief Clifford, reading a magazine as the aircraft took her away from the west coast of the United States. She looked out her window at the clouds below her and wondered how her life will be now that Andrea Canard was dead. The pursuit of that monster had all but consumed her since the murder of her father. She felt happy that it was finally over, but at the same time emotionally drained and ambivalent about the future. She put the magazine down on her lap and pinched the bridge of her nose in contemplation, trying to block out the engine noise. Just then she felt a hand gently touch her arm. Startled, she looked up. There stood a man, quite handsome, holding two glasses of red wine.

"*Excuse moi, belle dame,*" he spoke in fluid French, "but I could not help notice your distress and wondered if you would care to join me in a glass of wine ... it is a long flight and it may help you to relax," he smiled.

"How did you know I was French, *Monsieur?*" she asked.

The young man sat down next to her and handed her a glass. "Because, you must be," he smiled back. Simone returned the smile as they touched their glasses carefully together.

"My name is, *Jean Claude,*" he said.

"My name is, Simone," she responded.

"It is my pleasure to me you, Simone."

Simone nodded politely and drank. And then they talked and talked … the long miles away.

Chapter Thirty-Five

The *Gothic Gottfried* lay at anchor somewhere in the Yellow Sea, some miles off the coast of South Korea. Inside the plush main dining room, a small group of important looking men sat around a linen draped dinner table. Some of the guests wore military uniforms, while others expensive suits. They had just finished enjoying a delicious, before sunrise, dinner served by courteous waiters who had just removed the desert plates and were now serving drinks. A very large man at the head of the table lit up an imported cigar and then motioned with it for all the staff to exit the room. Once they had left and the table guests were alone, the large man dipped the unlit end of his cigar into his snifter of Remy Martin cognac, stirred several times, and then reinserted it into his large mouth. The other men sitting around the table smoked and sipped on their particular beverages, small talked, and waited patiently. After a while a man entered the room, unannounced. He went straight to the large man at the head of the table, whispered something into his ear, and he then quickly turned and left the room. The large man looked at his guests, smiled broadly, and announced: "Gentlemen, it has begun."

On hearing this, the men applauded at the news, a few toasting one another and offering words of congratulations.

"What are the particulars, Mr. Smith?" one oriental guest asked.

"Well, sir, an hour or so ago, the Korean People's Army crossed the thirty-eighth parallel near the Ongjin Peninsula. If all goes according to plan, we should own the entire Korean Peninsula within the year," Smith said, puffing on his cigar.

"And the Americans?" another asked.

"Unprepared. However, given their arrogance, and their unbridled hatred of all things communist, we predict that they will enter the fray in the fall. By that time, however, we will be fully entrenched, especially in the North," Smith answered with authority.

"Comrade Smith, we understand that a major shipment of medical supplies from the American west coast was confiscated. Will this impact our control over the South?" a uniformed man with a think Russian accent asked as he lit up a cigarette.

Smith drew a long breath, but smiled again pleasantly, pretending to be unaffected by the question.

"Indeed, comrade. I must say your intelligence network would seem to rival my own," Smith chuckled. However, you are mostly correct. A very substantial shipment of supplies did not make port in Busan. We shall have to wait and see how negative of an effect this will have on our schedule," Smith replied. "However, gentlemen," he continued, leaning forward, "let me be quite clear and assure you on this point," he paused to look at each one, "at this present time we are in full control of the North and will continue to be so for decades to come."

After the guests had left to return to their state rooms, Smith found himself on the forward deck, enjoying the Southeast Asian sunrise. He stood looking out over the water while heavy artillery fire was heard booming off in the distance like thunder. He smiled to himself as he lit up a cigarette. Suddenly, he became aware that he was not alone. He turned around to see a young woman approaching him. She was dressed, neck to feet, in black leather. Smith smiled and leaned into the railing for support. The woman's jet black hair blew freely in the mild breeze as she came up close to him, tipped her head in a salutation, and then looked out over the water.

"Welcome home, Miss Sato," Smith said, "I trust your mission went as expected?"

"Yumi Sato turned and looked up at Smith." He's dead. Did you require me to bring you his head?" she asked without emotion.

Smith shook his head slowly at her and chuckled, "No, indeed, just your assurance that the job is done will be sufficient.

Sato reached into her leather tunic, retrieved a small black box, and handed it to Smith.

"What's this?" Smith asked with a measure of surprise.

Sato just stood like a statue, motionless, and said nothing. Smith threw his cigarette overboard and then opened the box. Inside, resting on a cushioned liner was a severed ear.

"A gift, Miss Sato?" Smith inquired.

"A reminder, Mr. Smith ... in case you ever are given cause to doubt me in the future," she replied, as the slight wrinkle of a grin appeared momentarily at the corner of her mouth.

Smith laughed out loud now, nodding to her in appreciation, and then he tossed the box and its contents over the side. Afterward, they both leaned against the railing, listening to the shell bursts as if enjoying a concert.

"A question, if I may, Mr. Smith," Sato asked.

Smith turned his head towards her.

"Why were the tons of medical supplies shipped to this region so crucial?" she asked.

Smith grunted. "I wasn't aware that Circle politics interested you, Miss Sato?" Smith answered, somewhat surprised at her question.

"They do not. However, I am curious," she replied.

"Very well, my dear," Smith conceded, "the supplies in themselves are just that, medical supplies for field triage and for hospitals. They will need them to sustain the armies that are now in conflict. However, of real significance is what the supplies contain."

Sato gave Smith a puzzled look. Smith chuckled.

"You see, Miss Sato, it is all laced with, shall we say, our very special chemicals. The medicines, bandages, everything ... even the blood supply will soon be."

"And these chemicals are designed to do what?"

Smith stood up straight, stretched, and then yawned like a bull elephant.

"Why to make the masses obedient, Miss Sato. Control the mind and you control everything," he said, tapping a finger against his temple and rumbling with laughter.

Sato looked at Smith, seemingly unaffected by his explanation. Afterward, she gazed back again at the sea surrounding them. After a few more minutes, she said, "By the way, that woman, the detective's wife, Maxine? She's delivered a child, a girl. You had mentioned her before. I thought you should know."

Smith looked somewhat awestruck at the news, by reaching out and placing a chubby hand on Sato's shoulder. "What are you saying? Are you sure?"

Yumi Sato turned and looked at the hand resting on her shoulder, then back at Smith, her dark eyes smoldering. Smith quickly removed his hand and waited.

"Of course I'm sure," she replied firmly. "Now, if there's nothing else, Mr. Smith, I have a launch waiting. I'm needed in Tokyo."

Smith nodded to her in dismissal. Sato bowed deeply at the waist, turned, and left Smith standing again by himself.

Smith watched her walk away, and then he returned his attention back to the scenery ... the outline of a mainland in conflict, and the sounds of heavy weapons in the distance. But his mind was no longer focused on the present or future course of a regional war, but on the news he had just received. Gottfried Smith leaned against the railing of his ship, lit up another imported cigarette, and pondered out loud:

"Well now, we shall have to see about this matter."

Made in the USA
Columbia, SC
08 November 2023